THE GIRLS
OF CANBY HALL

ROOMMATES

EMILY CHASE

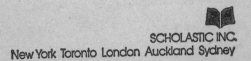

SCHOLASTIC INC.
New York Toronto London Auckland Sydney

ISBN 0–590–40078–9

12 11 10 9 8 7   6 7 8 9/8 0 1/9

THE GIRLS OF CANBY HALL®

ROOMMATES

THE GIRLS OF CANBY HALL

1

CHAPTER ONE

Dana Morrison sat in the far backseat of the van that had been sent from Canby Hall to pick up arriving students at the train station. There were five other girls crammed in with her, plus all their luggage in the back.

Dana thought, *This is what the pioneers must have felt like in their Conestoga wagons, packed in with all their belongings, setting off to a new life.*

Although Greenleaf, Massachusetts, about an hour north of Boston, was a big change from Manhattan, it was hardly wilderness territory. And the van ride was not exactly a major trek. It was only a mile from the station to the campus of Canby Hall, the boarding school Dana was transferring to in

1

this, her sophomore year; but the feeling of setting off on a new life was real.

The other girls in the van were all returning students. They were chatting away about what they'd done over the summer and how awful it was to have to be going back to school. Nobody really sounded all that unhappy about it, though. Dana guessed that, inside, they felt as she did. Every September, she was a little sorry that vacation was ending, but mostly she was getting tired of it and was looking forward to starting a fresh school year, with new pens and unwritten-in notebooks and untried teachers and courses in which she might get all *A*'s. (Anything could happen in a course she hadn't taken yet.)

In spite of being in such close company, Dana felt terribly lonely in the van. Everyone seemed to know everyone else and to have such an easy familiarity with the school. The girls were joking about it at the moment, the way people do about things they really like but don't want to seem too sentimental about.

They were talking about how dismal it was to be going back to Canby Hall food, and one particularly awful casserole they called Slime and Slide.

"What's in it?" Dana asked.

"Well, that's hard to say," one of the girls said. "On different days, it has different symptoms. If it's bad enough, they call in the nurse to take a look at it."

Dana laughed but she felt so out of it. Slime and Slide was just one of a million things all the other sophomores were already going to know about, and she wouldn't.

As the van pulled through the tall iron gates of the campus with its discreet brass plaque reading CANBY HALL, and up the tree-lined drive to Main Building, all Dana could think was, *What have I let myself in for?*

Dana had wakened at dawn that morning and tried to go back to sleep but couldn't.

There was no reason to be up this early. She'd packed everything the day before — except her toothbrush, blow-dryer, and the clothes she was planning to wear on the trip. The train didn't leave until one-thirty, which was over seven hours off.

After her umpteenth toss and turn, she gave up and got out of bed. She looked around the room. The side where her thirteen-year-old sister Maggie was sleeping still looked normal. Well, normal for Maggie, which meant the walls were covered with posters and magazine photos of Mick Jagger, her favorite rock star. Dana's side, with all her things stripped off the walls — her post-card collection of famous paintings, her programs from plays she'd gone to see — looked as bleak and bare as a prison cell.

This was too depressing. She went through her trunk and two giant suitcases and finally found her running gear. She got into shorts and a T-shirt and pulled her long brown hair into a rubber band at the base of her neck. She stretched her long legs with three sets of warm-up exercises. She put on her maroon running shoes, slid her apartment key into the little case that attached to the laces, and slipped silently out of the apartment so as not to wake Maggie or her mother. She ran down the eight flights rather than wait for the elevator.

"Hey, Smitty," she called to the doorman as she passed him at a sprint and burst out of the building into the very beginning of a perfect Indian summer day in New York City.

She ran her usual two-mile circuit at an easy lope. She wasn't interested in the run so much as the passing scene. She wanted to really *see* everything today, imprint the neighborhood on her mind. Now that she was leaving all this behind, even places she hardly ever noticed suddenly seemed important — landmarks of a life she was already beginning to miss, even though she was still here.

Goldman's Dry Cleaners, which was really owned by a Pakistani family that had taken over when old Mr. Goldman retired. Balducci's, which had the best tomatoes and avocados and sweet corn in all of New York City. The ice cream shop. The sign in the window said this month's special flavor was Banana Mint. Well, at least that was one thing she wouldn't miss.

But how was she going to survive without the Mandarin Chinese take-out place; the Punk Funk resale shop; Hartman's Bookstore, with its giant magazine rack where they didn't mind if you hung out for hours, as long as you didn't have a Fudgsicle in your hand? What was Greenleaf, Massachusetts, going to have to compare with all this?

Not that she was an urban snob. At least, she didn't think she was. But she knew she was a city girl at heart, and that the change was going to be a dramatic one. To her, trees were what grew in Central Park. Greenleaf was going to be *a lot* of trees, and probably not much else.

This was the first time she'd had such thoughts. Until today, she'd only been excited about going to Canby Hall. It was flattering to have been accepted at a school with such a good reputation. She was eager to live on a campus, in a dorm. She was a little nervous about having to make all new friends, but looking forward at the same time to meeting girls from all over the country. And there was a boys' school practically next door.

It wasn't until that morning that the whole thing suddenly seemed terrifying and ridiculous — to leave behind everything and everybody she loved for a total unknown.

"I've sort of changed my mind about going," she said to her mother when she got back to the apartment. Dana knew her mom was awake, even though she was in bed, under the covers, with her eyes closed. She was breathing like an awake person.

Edging her over, Dana sat down on the bed, being careful not to spill any of the huge bowl of granola and peaches that she was eating.

"You'll spoil your brunch," her mother said, thereby admitting to being awake. "We're supposed to meet your father at Grand Central at noon. What time is it anyway?"

"After seven," Dana said.

"How much after seven? I hope it's at least an hour after seven. I hope you're not waking me up before eight on a Saturday."

"I could tell you were up already," Dana said.

"Only sort of. I was drifting. But I value my drift time almost as much as my sleep time." Her mother yawned widely.

Dana's mother was a fashion buyer for a big department store and put in long hours during the week, trying to move up the ladder of success. Weekends, she liked to get up gradually, lounging and reading newspapers and having coffee and bagels. This usually took until noon.

"Did you hear me say I'd changed my mind about going?" Dana asked nervously.

"Yes, but I'm pretending I didn't. Can I have some of your granola?" Her mother reached for the bowl.

"Sure. Won't you listen to me about this? Please?" Dana begged.

"Okay."

"Now that it's time to go, I just don't think I can do it. I just don't think life in the woods is for me. All trees look alike to me. All birds are of a feather as far as I'm concerned. I'm not interested in listening to a babbling brook. I want to hear a subway rumbling by under my feet." Dana took back the bowl of granola.

"You talk as though you've just signed up to be a forest ranger. You're just going to school in a small town. I've heard rumors that civilization has gotten as far as Massachusetts. I don't think they wear pelts and live in caves anymore." Her mother smiled.

"You're making fun of me. I'm serious," Dana said.

"Well, I guess I think that's the best thing to do with these particular fears. They're just last-minute whim-whams, honey. Everybody gets them just before leaping into a big change. Brides, for instance, often get horrible jitters on their wedding days. *I* did. In that case, I probably should've listened to my nervous system."

"Oh, Mom," Dana said. She hated when her mother talked this way.

"Well, you have to admit the marriage was not a spectacular success. You notice they didn't make a warm, loving TV show about it: *Little Apartment on the Island*." Her mother reached for her robe at the bottom of the bed.

"It could still happen," Dana said encouragingly.

"I'm not discussing *that* one again. Especially before I've had my coffee. And as for your whim-whams, I think you just have to ignore them. Whatever you're thinking about Canby Hall will all change within five minutes of your getting there. Maybe you'll love it. Maybe you'll hate it. Probably both. But you won't know anything until you get there. And if you really do hate it, you can always come back. It isn't Devil's Island."

"I suppose you're right," Dana said, sighing. "Anyway, it's probably too late to back out now."

"You're darn right it is." This comment came from Maggie, who had apparently been standing in the doorway listening. "I've already bought the paint to redo the bedroom. Unless you're prepared to live with lime and fuschia, you might as well split for Massachusetts."

"Well," Dana laughed, "I guess that decides it."

In the taxi on the way to Grand Central, Dana's worries and thoughts about Canby Hall got pushed into the background. She and her mother were going to meet Dana's dad for a send-off breakfast. This was an event. Since their divorce, Dana's parents did not, as a rule, socialize with each other. When they did get together over something involving Dana or Maggie, they were very tense with each other. Dana hoped — although she had to admit it didn't seem like a very realistic hope — that the tension came out of their secretly still loving each other. Every time some occasion came up that was big enough for them to meet, Dana's hopes for their getting back together surged up all over again.

Her father was waiting in front of the coffee shop when they got there. He was leaning against the window, looking very casual in old jeans and a beat-up leather bomber jacket. He always dressed like that, funky but sharp — like the advertising copywriter he was. Dana liked this about him, although she loved him so much she knew she would still be crazy about him if he wore striped Bermudas and plaid shirts and a beanie with a propeller on top.

"Hi, you two," he said as they approached, but he was only looking at Dana. One of the many small difficulties her parents seemed to have was looking each other in the eye.

"So," he said to Dana when they had slid into a booth, he and Dana on one side, her mother on the other. "Your last real breakfast for a while. I think they only serve bowls of gruel at boarding schools. At least that's what they ate at boarding schools in Victorian novels."

"What's gruel?" Dana asked, furrowing the brows over her large green eyes.

"Like porridge, I think. Only more watery. They only serve that at breakfast, though. For lunch and dinner, they serve greasy mutton stew," her father said, trying to look serious.

"What's mutton?" Dana asked.

"Oh, never mind," he said, but not impatiently. "Actually, you're probably just going to have to face standard institutional cooking, which is to say you'll think it's awful *and* you'll gain ten pounds from it."

"Oh, no!" Dana said.

"Don't worry, kiddo. If there's anyone who can afford a few extra pounds, it's you." Then he turned to Dana's mother as if he'd just realized she was sitting across the table. "How's it going, Carol?"

From there, the two of them were off and running. Stopping only to order when the waitress came around, they snapped at each other through the whole meal. Not fighting exactly, just taking little jabs at every opportunity.

By the time Dana got on the train, she was good and mad. For the first fifty miles or so, all she could think of was that her parents had been so involved in their own drama at the restaurant that they had pretty much ignored her, denied her *her* moment of importance.

She got deep into a warm fantasy about the four of them — her mom and dad and she and Maggie — having a Christmas like the ones they used to, when everyone got each other one real gift and one joke gift, and they went out to a Mexican or Chinese restaurant for Christmas dinner, just to be untraditional.

Then she fell asleep.

When she woke up, the train was pulling into the Greenleaf station. Out the window, she could see a van with CANBY HALL lettered on its side.

CHAPTER TWO

While Dana was in the van coming out to Canby Hall, Faith Thompson was already up in Baker House, Room 407, unpacking. She had come up on a morning train and had already checked in, gotten her room key, bed linen, and what seemed like millions of mimeographed sheets of information about orientation lectures, class schedules, meal hours, bicycle parking regulations (she didn't even have a bike!) and so on.

When she had first gotten to the room, followed closely by one of the guys from nearby Oakley Prep, who were serving as luggage haulers for the day, she just shut the door behind her and collapsed on the nearest bed.

In a few minutes her head stopped spinning and she looked around. She was apparently the first one here. There was no other luggage besides hers, no signs of human life. The room was stripped bare of any traces of whoever had lived there last year. The walls had been painted and the floors waxed over the summer.

Without any decorations, it was a pretty grim place. Three beds, three bureaus, three small desks with chairs and lamps and wastebaskets. One old easy chair in the corner. At the windows, there were the fat, old, yellowed kind of venetian blinds, but no curtains. The color on the walls was what Faith thought of as insane-asylum green — sort of the color of a dead mint leaf. She had brought up her own bedspread — a brown and orange print. *This is going to look totally gross in here*, she thought.

The room was bigger than the one she shared with her older sister Sarah at home. But there were going to be three of them in here, and all of them strangers to each other. It suddenly seemed impossible that she would be able to stand living in such bleak surroundings, much less with two girls she had never met. Probably both white girls at that. She had never shared a room with a white girl before.

All of a sudden, Faith was scared. She felt like staying there and curling up on the bed. But she made herself get up and start unpacking all her clothes and books and camera equipment. And as she made some order out of the chaos around her and began to put some of her things around the room, she felt a little better. *It's going to be okay, girl*, she told herself. *Whatever this place has to hand out, you're just going to roll with it.*

When Faith's alarm had gone off that morning, it jolted her up from the depths of sleep. She woke with disbelief. It felt as if she had been asleep only for an hour, but the clock unmistakably read nine, and the sunlight pouring in through her bedroom window was already bright. A light breeze was rippling the sheer white curtains, but the air was already filled with the heat of the day to come. Even though it was the first week in September, summer was still hanging suffocatingly over Washington, D.C.

It'll probably be cooler around Boston, Faith thought.

Why am I so tired at nine in the morning? she wondered, as she started to get out of bed. Then she remembered the night before. The party.

What a party. *Her* going-away party. No girl could have asked for a better send-off. It had been huge. Sabrina, Faith's best friend, had it at her place and invited everyone important to Faith.

Faith's family had come, of course. Her older sister Sarah, her little brother Richard, her mother. It was a potluck supper, and so everyone brought something. Sabrina had made a giant cake shaped like a schoolhouse. Written on it in frosting was "Go to the head of the class, Faith." Everyone was really proud of Faith for winning a scholarship to a school like Canby Hall.

Basically, Faith was happy to be going. Not that she was particularly rah-rah or gung ho. Faith was hardly ever rah-rah about anything. Sarah had told her a while back that Faith was the least excitable, most practical-minded fifteen-year-old she'd ever seen.

But Canby Hall did fit in with Faith's life plan. Going to an impressive school would probably make it easier for her to get into photography at one of the good art colleges. Faith was determined that, by the time she was twenty-five, she was going to be a top news photographer. Then she'd think about finding a guy and combining her career with marriage and kids. Like her mother.

She wasn't crazy about leaving her mom and brother and sister and a life in Washington that was good, but she couldn't be sentimental if she was going to get where she was going.

Actually, most of her sentimentality had dried up after her father had been killed two years before. He was a policeman who had been trying to stop a bank robbery when he was shot — four times. In the year or so following his death, Faith had cried what she guessed was her lifetime supply of tears. When she ran out, that was it. She hadn't cried since. About anything. Her heart was like a stone inside her.

She forced herself out of bed and padded downstairs to the kitchen to try to dig up something resembling breakfast. But then, standing in front of the open refrigerator, she decided that frying up eggs and bacon, toasting toast, and making coffee was a lot more trouble than she could handle in her half-awake state.

She shut the fridge door and ran back upstairs. After showering and washing her hair, she pulled a pair of jeans onto her thin legs and narrow hips, shrugged into a tank top, fluffed up her short Afro, stuffed a few dollars into her pocket, and went out into the morning.

She walked through the heat down to George's Diner. When she came in, she was greeted by a blissful blast of air conditioning and a curious look from George.

"Girl," he said, "aren't you supposed to be off to that fancy school today?"

"In an hour or so. I'm all packed. I've got to catch a cab out to the station. Can you fix me my favorite breakfast of champions?" Faith asked as she sat down at the counter.

"Okay. One double cheeseburger, fries, and a strawberry shake coming up."

He slapped the patties and bun on the grill, tossed the fries into the deep fat, whirred the shake through the blender, and came back and leaned on the counter.

"So where's your send-off crew? Nobody around to break a bottle of champagne on you like you were a ship?" he asked.

"No. Sarah's got classes at Georgetown. Richard's back in school already. Mom thought she could go to the station with me, but at the last minute she got called to testify at a custody hearing. Social workers are a lot at the mercy of the schedules of judges and lawyers. I don't mind. I figure the party was my send-off. Today, I'd just as soon slip away without a lot of mushy farewell stuff."

"Yeah, yeah. We all know how tough you are. Say. Aren't you at least a little excited to be going up to this school?" George wiped the counter casually.

She never was very good at lying to George. He'd been a friend of the family ever since she was born, and he had always had a way of getting to what was really going on with her.

Fiddling with the sugar container so she wouldn't have to look George straight in the eye, Faith said, "I guess I'm more scared than anything. I think it's mostly going to be white girls up there, and I just don't know too much about what they're like. Different from me, though, I'll bet."

"Oh, you'll do fine. You've got a way with people. You'll knock 'em dead," George said, giving her shoulder a little shake of encouragement.

"Maybe I don't want to. I don't know if

I'm going to even particularly like anybody up there. I don't think white kids have the same sense of humor I do. Oh, I don't know. It's all so strange, I don't even know what to start worrying about. So I guess I won't bother to start at all. I've got name tags sewn into all my clothes, my bags waiting in the hallway, my train ticket bought. I guess I'll have to take the rest as it comes."

When Faith was done unpacking, she went to the window and looked out over the campus. Hardly any of the students had arrived yet. It seemed eerily neat and clean and quiet, like a picture on the back of a postcard. It was for sure nothing like her neighborhood back home, which was always alive in the summer with the combined noise of radios and kids on Hot Wheels and the chimes of the Melody Freeze truck.

She turned away from the window and spotted an envelope of negatives she had shot last week. She picked it up and sat down on her bed, figuring this was as good a time as any to sort through them.

When she was in the middle of this, a tall, thin girl — real cute with long shiny brown hair and bright green eyes — pushed the door open hesitantly and came into the room. Faith noticed that she was wearing designer jeans and an expensive polo shirt — the kind of clothes Faith could only afford imitation versions of. When the Oakley guy who was helping with the luggage set it all down, it looked to be about as much as a movie star would bring on a publicity tour.

The girl smiled.

"Hi," she said, "I'm Dana Morrison."

"Faith Thompson."

"I guess we're roommates. Your name's on here." Dana looked down at the card in her hand.

"Are you a sophomore?" Faith asked.

"Yes, but it's my first year here. I'm a transfer."

"Me, too."

"That's probably why they put us in together. Has the third girl" — Dana looked down at the card again — "Michelle Hyde, shown up?"

"Not yet." Faith knew they both were nervous.

"You know," Dana said, "on the way up the stairs, I was wondering what you two would be like."

"I'm probably not what you expected." Faith said.

"No. I thought you'd have long blond hair and crooked teeth and write tragic poetry." Dana smiled briefly.

Faith laughed. "Well, sometimes I take tragic pictures. These here, for instance, are pretty bad."

"Are you a photographer?" Dana asked.

"Sort of," Faith said, not wanting to sound self-important.

"Neat," Dana said. "I sing and write songs. Not very tragic ones. And I play guitar."

"I gathered," Faith said, nodding toward the guitar case among Dana's luggage. "I didn't think that was your machine gun."

Dana laughed. "Hey. I can't bear the idea of getting down to all this unpacking. What do you say we go out and take a look around this joint?"

"Oh, I don't think so," Faith said, not wanting to get too friendly too fast with this rich girl. "I think I'm heading into a major nap. I had quite a night last night." Then she realized that this sounded as if she'd been at some wild disco into the wee hours instead of at a potluck supper with her family. Oh, well, let this girl think she led life in the fast lane. It would give Faith an air of mystery.

"Hey," Faith called out as Dana was shutting the door behind herself on her way out. Dana poked her head back in. "If you're not back by the time I get up, I'll send out a St. Bernard for you."

CHAPTER
THREE

While Faith and Danā were talking, Shelley Hyde was still a way off from Canby Hall, on the Greyhound bus from Boston, where she had flown from her home in Iowa.

On the bus, she wound up seated next to another girl on her way to Canby Hall. The girl's name was Maureen, and she was a sophomore like Shelley but not a transfer. She had spent her freshman year at Canby Hall. Maureen had red hair and freckles and the cheeriest disposition Shelley had ever run across.

"You'll really like it there," she assured Shelley. "It's really a cool school. The classes are sort of tough, but most of the teachers are good. Not boring. And I like the girls there. I come from a small town in Pennsylvania where everyone is more or less like me. I was getting a little tired of that. At Canby Hall, there are all different types. It's real interesting. And there's lots of fun stuff to do. Something's always happening. I think you'll really like it. You've just got to stay out of trouble."

"Oh," Shelley said, "I don't think I'll be getting into any trouble. But I don't really think I'll be getting involved much with Canby Hall either. I'm sure it's a swell place and all, but, well — my heart's really back in Pine Bluff."

"Oh." Maureen nodded knowingly. "A boyfriend."

Shelley just smiled shyly. She couldn't help smiling when the subject of Paul came up.

"Well," Maureen said, "the funny thing is, those back-home boyfriends tend to fade away when they're a thousand miles off."

"Not this one," Shelley said, with no smile this time. Maureen might be nice, but she clearly didn't understand at all.

Shelley's day had started so early that it was still half-dark when she sat next to Paul, his arm draped over her shoulder as he drove. They sat in silence as his car cruised along the highway out of town, through the cornfields that looked blue in the predawn light.

She disengaged herself from him, slid across the front seat, and leaned against the door on the other side.

"Hey. Where'd my girl go?" he said, not taking his eyes off the road.

"I want to get a good look at you," she said. "I especially like watching you when you're doing something and can't watch me back."

"That doesn't make me *too* self-conscious or anything," he said with a grin.

"Oh, come on. Let me be sentimental this morning. I've got one hour left of you to last me three months." Shelley's voice caught.

"You don't *have* to be going to Candy Hall, you know," he said.

"You know it's *Canby* Hall. And you also know how much say I have around my house when my parents work up to a united-front decision."

"I still don't understand why they have to ship you halfway across the country when we've got one of the best high schools in the state right here." Paul's hands tightened on the wheel.

"I'm not sure either. I told you, they keep saying that this is going to 'broaden my horizons.' But I think it's really about you and me." Shelley glanced at Paul's handsome profile.

"I thought they liked me. I'm clean-cut. I was a boy scout. My intentions are honorable."

"Of course they like you. But they also think *I* like you too much for my own good. I think they think that if I stay here around you, I'm going to wind up married with three kids by the time I'm old enough to vote. And that I'll never get around to college. To them, college is the third most important event for anyone — right after birth and death."

They drove the rest of the way out to the bluff in silence. They were going there so they could say their good-byes in private, not at the bus depot later with her whole family there. Shelley looked at Paul the whole time. She never got tired of looking at him. She thought he was the best-looking guy in Pine Bluff. And the smartest. And the funniest. After going with him for a whole year, she sometimes still went weak in the knees when he surprised her by unexpectedly coming around a corner in the corridor at school, or when he came to pick her up for a date.

She couldn't believe it when he first asked her out. He could have had his pick of the most beautiful and popular girls at Polk High. Not that she thought she was a wretch or anything. She liked having blond hair and blue eyes, but thought of herself as cute rather than beautiful. She was a little too chunky. More than almost anything, she would have liked to win the battle against spaghetti and chocolate cake, and lose the fifteen pounds she felt was standing between the Shelley who existed now and the thin and lovely girl she dreamed of being.

She hated leaving Paul. She knew she would be miserable without him. If her parents thought this separation was going to split them up, they were wrong. Shelley had packed nearly half a suitcase of stationery and stamps. She intended to write Paul every single day. Maybe when her folks saw that the separation was only strengthening their relationship, they would finally understand that this was not just puppy love.

Once they got to the bluff, dawn was just

breaking over the farmland below. This was their favorite spot. It was one of the few real views around their particularly flat part of Iowa.

They sat side by side in the long grass. They didn't say much. There really wasn't much left that hadn't already been said. For Shelley, it was both a sad and a strangely beautiful moment. She had never felt quite so close to him. And he wasn't touching her, not even looking at her. He was just so *there* next to her.

Somehow, she managed not to cry in front of Paul, even when he kissed her good-bye. But as soon as he dropped her off, she ran straight up to the bathroom, sat down on the edge of the tub, and began to sob. She thought everyone else in the house was still asleep. Then she heard a floorboard creaking outside the door. Then everything was silent again, and she felt safe and alone enough to let go with another deluge.

"Hey," someone said suddenly from the other side of the door. "Is the plumbing broken, or are you making all that noise by yourself, Slugger?" (Her brothers had given her this nickname years ago when she was trying to learn to play softball.)

Shelley knew it was her brother Jeff outside. She opened the door to find him standing there, trying hard not to crack a smile. He couldn't, and neither could she. In the middle of her smile, she thought how terrific Jeff was and how much she'd miss him, too, and surprised both of them by bursting into another round of tears.

"Gee, are you a mess, kid," he said. "What are you going to do on the plane? I hope they've got crying and noncrying sections."

For breakfast, her mom fixed all of Shelley's favorites — lots of pancakes with melted butter and warm syrup, the really good bacon old Mr. Hodges cured in the smokehouse behind his butcher shop, and fresh-squeezed orange juice.

"How long's it going to take you to get there?" her brother Larry asked her.

"What are you talking about, Larry?" Jeff said. "She's not going to make it all the way out there. We're talking about Slugger, the girl who once got lost on her way to the school bus stop."

"Come *on*," Shelley protested. "That was when I was five."

But Jeff couldn't be stopped.

"No way she's going to make it all the way

through a trip that involves two buses and a plane. Sometime around the middle of October, we're going to get a call from somewhere in Ohio. Maybe western Pennsylvania, but that's the limit."

"You guys are really making me feel terrific. I guess that's what families are for, though, to boost a girl's confidence. Listen, if you want me to stay, I'd be only too glad." Shelley really meant it.

"Now, now," her dad said, "none of that talk."

Aside from being furious with him for sending her off like this, Shelley was crazy about her dad. About her mom, too. She was one of the few girls she knew who thought growing up to be just like her parents would be perfectly okay. And she thought it was sweet that her parents had been married twenty-two years and were still as in love with each other as honeymooners.

Whenever she thought of herself in adult life, it was a life much like theirs. Except she and Paul would have a brick barbecue and a swimming pool out back of *their* house.

So, if she was perfectly content to stay in Pine Bluff for the rest of her life, why did she have to be uprooted and transplanted to

Massachusetts? When they sprung this on her, she hadn't even known exactly where Massachusetts was. (She had always fallen asleep in geography.) She knew it was east somewhere, but had to get out the atlas to see exactly where.

She knew Canby Hall was a good school, and it looked like a pretty campus from the pictures in the brochure. But what was she supposed to get out of going there that she couldn't get right there at Polk High? She did fine in school and knew just what she wanted to do afterward. She was even willing to go to college to please her folks. She'd go to State with Paul. While he was studying business, she'd major in home economics. All of this was so clear and logical in her head. It seemed like the only possible effect Canby Hall could have on her would be to get her confused about these perfectly good plans.

In Pine Bluff, Shelley had only hated the *idea* of Canby Hall. Now, sitting here on the bus next to Maureen, who had fallen silent after Shelley had cut her off on the subject of Paul, she began to fear the *place*.

By the time the bus pulled into the depot

at Greenleaf, she had worked up a whole list of terrors:

Because she was transferring as a sophomore, all the other girls in her class would have been there a year already and know each other, and she would be an outsider.

The other girls would be from cities and dress more stylishly than she did.

They'd use a lot of slang she wouldn't understand.

They'd think she was a hick.

Added to her fears was the way she felt when she finally got to Greenleaf — exhausted, gritty, and headachy from all the Cokes and Snickers she'd had during the long day. By the time she got her room assignment and was tromping up the four flights, all she wanted out of life was a toothbrush and a bed.

She looked down at the three-by-five card in her hand and read:

407—BAKER HOUSE
HYDE, MICHELLE
MORRISON, DANA
THOMPSON, FAITH

Seeing her own name above those of two total strangers gave her an unexpected jolt. These were the names of real people who, like them or not, she was going to be spending the next year with.

When she got to the top of the last flight of stairs, she was in a long, wide hallway.

It was an odd sensation. There was no one in the hall. Its wood floors glowed softly in the dim overhead lights. She could hear the rush of water from a nearby shower, three or four radios or stereos playing different music, the high buzz of a blow-dryer, and frequent bursts of laughter.

She looked for room numbers and found them stenciled on the doors. She was going the wrong way. She turned around and headed back. 411, 409, 407. *This was it*. The door was ajar. She stood in front of it for a minute, considering whether or not to knock, then decided she might as well just go on in. It was, after all, *her* door.

She had expected to find her two roommates already there, but there was only one other girl in the room. She was lying on the bed in the far corner, but sat up as Shelley came into the room.

"Hi," the girl said. "You must be Michelle.

The rest of us are all accounted for. I'm Faith Thompson."

Shelley returned the hi and said yes, she was Michelle, but everyone called her Shelley. She hoped she was managing to get through this initial chitchat without looking as astounded as she felt to find that this roommate of hers was a black girl.

There were about a dozen black people in Pine Bluff, but she didn't know any of them. Faith Thompson was going to be the first black person she had ever really known in her life. While this was interesting, she wondered if they'd have much to say to each other.

She hoped she wasn't letting all this show on her face, but from Faith's increasingly suspicious look, Shelley suspected she probably was. Then she knew for certain she was in trouble when Faith said, "Do I have my nose on backward or something?"

"N-no," Shelley stammered. "Why?"

"You sure are looking at me funny." Faith's voice was tight.

"Oh. Sorry. I — uh — I just didn't expect you to be so — short."

"I'm five-ten," Faith said dryly. "I just look a lot shorter when I'm sitting down."

Shelley got more nervous. She thought, *Well, the truth is probably somewhat better than any more of the feeble lies I could come up with.*

"I was just surprised that you're black," Shelley finally said nervously.

"Is it such a big deal?" Faith asked, defensively.

"Oh, no. I don't know many black people, but"— Shelley thought for a second about how to finish the sentence — "but I'm sure they can be as nice as anyone else."

She knew the words had come out all wrong as soon as she said them, but it was too late to take them back. She couldn't think of how to get her foot out of her mouth without putting the other one in. She was afraid to try again for fear something even stupider would pass her lips.

Faith's eyes were bright with anger, and her voice was hurt and shaky as she said, "Yes. Sometimes, if we really try, we can even be as nice as you white folks."

With that, she stormed past Shelley and out the door.

She stomped down the stairs and out of Baker House. She spotted Dana sitting on one of the old wood benches on the front lawn, studying her campus map. Faith changed direction fast so Dana wouldn't see her. She didn't want to deal with anybody at the moment — especially anyone white.

CHAPTER FOUR

Dana didn't see Faith, and so had no idea how drastically wrong things had gone in the peaceful dorm room she had left just fifteen minutes before.

She was calm and happy and just sitting there stretching her long legs in front of her, resting her head on the back of the bench, enjoying the hazy late afternoon. Everything here looked so green, *smelled* so green.

Other students were arriving — some in the Canby Hall van from the train station, others by car with their parents. And these weren't all of them. Monday morning, the day students would come back and fill out their ranks.

As far as Dana could see, there didn't seem to be any such thing as the typical Canby

Hall girl. They seemed to come in all shapes and sizes. Two walked by her speaking French to each other, so she guessed they were not even all from this country.

There did seem to be something of a Canby Hall look though. The older girls — the ones who had been there a while — were wearing cords or good jeans, crew-necks or cardigans. They wore their hair shiny clean and well-cut. Their faces look scrubbed and not very made-up. Clearly, this wasn't a place where the old sweatshirt and heavy eyeliner look was in. Grubby was not the style here.

Dana had brought her Canby Hall handbook with her to look at the campus map inside. She skipped over the endless pages of rules. She could read them later. There sure were a lot. She had probably broken a dozen already.

She looked at the map, then around her, and tried to get her bearings. It was hopeless. She was the kind of person who couldn't figure out a map even to get out of a desert or to find buried treasure. She rolled up the book and stuck it in her back pocket in defeat. She would just have to wander around and hope she found her way back eventually.

She walked across the campus's central

park, past Main Building, where most classes
were held, the dining hall, the science building, and the library, which were all in a row.
Behind the library, she was surprised to find
a small orchard. She picked an apple from a
low-hanging branch and bit into it. There
was a wonderful explosion of flavor in her
mouth. Before she took a second bite,
though, she thought, *This is probably breaking some rule.*

Beyond the orchard was a farm with a
barnyard and stables with horses that
came up to the fence for nuzzling and for
the sugar Dana didn't have. She gave her
apple core to one of the colts.

Past the farm was a big house with a white
lattice gazebo on its lawn. She figured this
must belong to some school bigwig. The
headmistress, probably. Further along was
the chapel. If she made it into the choir, this
was where she would be doing her singing.

Around from there was the sports com-
plex — tennis courts, fieldhouse, playing
fields. She did a couple of slow, loping cir-
cuits around the cinder track, just to try it
out.

Then she went looking for Baker and,
amazingly, found it. She knew she hadn't
seen the whole of the campus. It was bigger

than she thought, but not so big that she was going to feel lost. That was good to know.

She approached Baker House from the front, and stopped to really look at her new home. It was, like most of the buildings on campus, built of red brick with white trim, and fairly buried under ivy. It was amazing that it was even still upright, given all the years of girls it had withstood. She pictured the first girls who had lived there when the school opened in 1897 — girls in long white dresses and straw hats with long, trailing ribbons. She imagined the girls of the 1920s with their boyish haircuts and middy blouses and long ropes of beads. She could see the girls of the Depression, coming to Canby wearing sensible shoes and blouses worn at the cuffs. Then the page-boyed girls whose boyfriends went off to World War II. Then the girls of the sixties in their bell-bottoms and tie-dyed shirts, who themselves went off to peace marches and protest rallies.

It was one of the first times in her life that Dana had thought about tradition. Starting today, she was part of one. She wondered if someday, some girl of a future generation would stand here and think back on Dana's generation. What would she imagine? What would Dana and her friends be remembered for? What would her friends here be like?

When Dana got back to the room, Faith was gone. But someone else *was* there — a short, slightly chubby, blond girl. She looked like a character from a fifties movie about teenagers, like she was just about to jump up and start jitterbugging. She was wearing a big white sweater in a kind of popcorn knit, a plaid pleated skirt, and white tennis shoes. The only missing ingredient was bobby socks. Her hair was smooth and puffy and curled under.

She was sitting scrunched over one of the desks, so intent on what she was writing that her forehead was almost touching the desk lamp. She was using a purple felt tip pen on pink parchment. *It must be a love letter*, Dana figured. She bet the paper was perfumed.

"Hi," Dana said to her.

Before the girl had a chance to answer, Faith came back into the room, brushed past Dana, threw herself on the bed with a sigh, opened a *People* magazine, and started reading — all without saying a word to anyone. Either she was more aloof than Dana had thought, or something was wrong between her and the new girl.

"Well," Dana forged on with the new girl, "by process of elimination, you must be Michelle."

"That's me. But everyone calls me Shelley," she said, then ran on nervously, "except my brothers. They call me Slugger. But please don't. I was really hoping I could leave that back in Iowa."

"Slugger," Faith said, going back to *People*. "Cute."

Dana couldn't tell if she was being sarcastic.

"It's so Norman Rockwell," Faith went on.

She *was* being sarcastic. Shelley picked up on the remark, but not on the tone.

"Oh," she said, "don't you think he's the greatest? His paintings are so *true*."

"Not *my* truth," Faith said.

"Oh," Shelley said, starting to blush, "you mean because they're about white people?"

"So," Dana interrupted nervously, "you're from Iowa?"

"Yeah. Pine Bluff. You've probably never heard of it. It's near Ames."

Dana hadn't heard of Ames either, but nodded as though she had.

"I'm from New York City," Dana said.

"Ooooh," Shelley said. "That must be exciting."

"And Faith's from Washington, D.C.," Dana went on.

"Oh," Shelley said, "I've been there." She turned toward Faith, who was not giving an inch. She was staring at her magazine, but Shelley plunged on.

"My family went there on vacation once. We saw the Lincoln Memorial, the Washington Monument, the White House, the Capitol, and the Mint."

"Yeah," Faith said, still not looking up, "that's where we live."

"Near the Mint?" Shelley asked.

"No — *in* the Mint. We live in the basement. It's okay. Except on days when they make nickels. Those nickels are really noisy."

"Well, that *is* interesting," Shelley said, her voice going from friendly and nervous to stone-cold dead. "And I live in a barn. And Dana probably lives on top of the Empire State Building with King Kong."

"Hey!" Dana leapt in. "I don't know about you two, but I'm hungry enough to eat a horse, which, according to what I hear, is probably what they're serving for dinner tonight. What say we go down together and get to know each other a little better?"

The other two looked at her as if she'd suggested they all take a tour of the campus sewer system, but they reluctantly agreed to go.

At dinner, things went from bad to worse, or at least stayed as bad as they were. The dining hall, which was next to Main Building, was a nice enough place. One whole side was windows facing a green meadow. Sunlight came through the windows, shining on the hanging green plants. A salad bar was along one wall and a long cafeteria line had formed across the back of the hall. Canby girls quickly got their plates, giggling about the food. The rest of the hall was filled with round oak tables and matching chairs. The hall was so noisy with the chatter of girls and the clatter of plates that the girls had to talk loudly, which put quite a cramp in their already faltering conversation.

Dana tried to get things off personal topics, to get everyone in a kidding-around frame of mind. She decided to pick on the stew, which had been listed in the cafeteria menu as "Kentucky Surprise."

"What'd I tell you," she said, "about eating a horse? I mean, I ask you, what do they have an awful lot of in Kentucky that would be a real surprise in a stew?"

But neither of the other two were biting, either on Dana's jokes or on the stew. They both sat in silence, pushing peas and carrots and little hunks of stringy meat around on their plates. Dana thought, *This is worse than being on a first date, as far as getting a conversation going.*

She was getting a little tired of doing all the work, too. She could see at least the outlines of the problem. Something had gone dreadfully wrong before she even got back to the room. Faith wasn't a mean person. She was probably bristling in response to something Shelley had said or done. Since Shelley didn't seem like a nasty person either, the something had probably been unintentional. Dana guessed it was something about Faith being black. She also had the feeling the whole mess could be straightened out with a few words. But, not *really* knowing what the problem was, she couldn't come up with the solution.

And so, defeated, Dana joined in the general silence and gloom. She ate her stew — which was pretty bad, but probably not horse meat — and looked around at the girls at the other tables. She envied their talk and laughter. They were sliding easily into the rhythms of school life, while she was stuck with these two pillars of stone.

She'd been looking forward all summer to living in a dorm, and now it looked like she was going to have to live there saddled with two roommates who had apparently decided, on the basis of some minor-league snit, to hate each other forever. Terrific.

Then Dana started getting mad. Because of *their* problem, *her* fun was going to be spoiled. *Phooey on both of them*, she thought, thereby making the mutual un-admiration society a three-member club.

CHAPTER FIVE

Shelley was up the next morning a couple of hours before the other two. It was Sunday. Nothing was scheduled until the headmistress's welcoming address at two. The dorm floor was quiet. Everyone was still sleeping, but Shelley was used to getting up early— *and* eating a big breakfast. So she put on some slacks and a top and tiptoed out to the dining hall alone.

There weren't many girls there — maybe twenty or so other early risers. Shelley took a tray and went through the cafeteria line. Scrambled something (not quite eggs), dried little hockey pucks of sausage, toast that was spread with something that sat on the slices in pats reluctant to melt. So far, about the only good thing Shelley could see about Canby Hall was that she would probably lose some weight here.

Just looking at the room full of strangers made her eyes fill up with tears of longing to be back in Pine Bluff. She could just see her family sitting down to breakfast, eating great pancakes, cracking jokes.

The tears were running down her cheeks by the time she set her tray down on a nearby table. She didn't even look to see who was sitting there. She just pulled out an empty chair, sat down, and wiped her eyes with a paper napkin.

"Gee," somebody said. "This must be a new girl. She still has some standards. Now that I've been here three years, this food even seems sort of edible to me."

Shelley couldn't help smiling, even in the middle of her tears. The two girls at the table were older, clearly good friends. Although one was tall and big and blond and the other small with dark hair and olive skin, they both wore their hair in the same exact style — long and folded back with a brush and blow-dryer. Both were wearing corduroy pants, crew-necks, and oxford cloth shirts. Beyond these similarities, they just had that easy space floating between them of people who have known and liked each other for a long time. That made her think of Cindy Carver, her best friend back in Pine Bluff, which started her crying again.

"Sorry," Shelley said, when she was down to just sniffling. "It's just that everywhere I look around here, I see something that reminds me of home."

"Oh, boy," the blond said. "If you're this bad on Sunday morning, wait until tonight. Sunday nights are homesick heaven around here. Everybody gets really low. They play their most depressing country records, cry in their Tabs, and line up by the phones to call their parents."

"Who they'd probably be ignoring if they were home," the dark-haired girl said.

"Right. Sometimes I think our folks send us here just so we'll appreciate them more."

"It's not just my parents," Shelley said. "It's everything. My boyfriend, my brothers, my friends, my school, my bedroom. This morning I even missed my goldfish, Sam."

"A bad case," the blond said. "What you need is a little party to cheer you up. Get your roommates to order a pizza with you tonight. Play some old rock records and dance your troubles away. A lot of the girls do that. They call them Sunday Sliders — little parties to get you through the worst of it."

"I don't know about that," Shelley said. "I'm not getting along too well with my room- mates." She told them the story.

They both listened and then appeared to think about the matter. Finally, the dark- haired girl said, "You've got to do something to bring the three of you together. A project of some kind. Something you can do as a team."

Shelley never did learn the two girls' names. They were finished eating before she was, so she didn't talk to them much longer. It was nice to know, though, that not every- one around the place was difficult and hard to get along with.

When she got back to the room, she sat down at her desk and looked around. It was pretty grim, but with a few of the right touches, it might just possibly be a homey little spot.

That was it! Here was the team project! This was just the thing to get things back on track with the three of them. They could plan and decorate the room together. She bet they'd go for it. She figured neither of them wanted another night like the last one, when all three of them had gone to bed in stony silence.

She got out a pen and notebook and

started jotting down color schemes, making diagrams. By the time the other two woke up, she had a great plan all ready for presentation.

She waited until they had showered and dressed and looked more or less awake before springing it on them.

"Hey!" she announced, "I've come up with a terrific plan for the room!"

"What do you mean — plan?" Dana said warily.

"You know. A decorating scheme. You want the place to look homey, don't you?"

"Frankly," Faith said, "I don't care if it looks like cell block nine. I figure it's someplace to crack the books and crash at night."

"Yeah," Dana said, "no matter what you do to it, it's never going to be something out of a decorating magazine, so why bother?"

"But it won't be much work," Shelley protested. "Just a little style here. A little color there. I've worked it all out here," she said pointing to her notes.

"Oh," Faith said to Dana, "the girl's been cooking while we've been sleeping. But don't decorators usually ask you what you want? Do they usually just go ahead and figure you'll either like it or lump it?"

"Wait a minute," Shelley said. "These are

just rough ideas. I mean I *want* to know what you think. You can change anything you don't like."

"Oh, come on, Faith," Dana said. "What've we got to lose by listening? I'm interested, Shelley. Really I am."

Dana had been standing in the middle of the room, bent over, rubbing her long wet hair in a towel. She wound the towel up into a turban and sat down on the edge of her bed, like a student getting ready for a lecture.

Faith flopped down on her bed like a child who'd been naughty and told to stay put for a minute.

"Whatever you want to do," she said, "I probably haven't got the money for it anyway."

"Oh," Shelley said, "it won't cost hardly a cent. Really. My mother has tons of fabric remnants, and she's a whiz on the Singer. She can stitch up the café curtains and dust ruffles and pillow shams in no time."

"Dust ruffles?" Dana said.

"Pillow shams?" Faith said.

"Well, see," Shelley said. "I sort of had in mind a country cottage look. Lots of flower prints. Chintz dust ruffles. Eyelet lace curtains." She stopped. Both Dana and Faith were staring at her, their mouths slightly open and speechless.

"Uh," Dana finally said, then looked over at Faith, as if for help.

"Well," Faith started. She didn't finish.

Shelley waited for either of them to say *anything*, but neither one did. They hated her idea, it was clear. They thought her taste was terrible — so bad they couldn't find even one nice thing to say. How could they do this to her? Even if they didn't like the idea, couldn't they see it was really just her way of trying to patch things up?

She felt hot tears filling her eyes. She didn't want them to see that she was crying, though, so she ran out of the room, and down the hall. As she ran, she heard a burst of laughter behind her. She couldn't be sure it was them. It could have come from another room. No, it was probably them. Sharing some sickening joke about what hayseed taste she had.

She ran into the bathroom. Luckily, no one else was in there. The five sinks were unused, for once. The showers and johns were empty. Shelley ran cold water and splashed it on her face until she no longer felt on fire.

She hated them — both of them. She wouldn't speak to either one of them ever again. Ever. She felt a little better just thinking how uncomfortable this would make them, if she could keep it up.

She looked in the mirror. Her eyes were still puffy, her cheeks still a little flushed. She slipped out of the dorm without going back to the room. She wanted to wait until she was completely calm and composed before she faced them again — silently. They thought she was a wimp, but they were wrong. A month or so of her frostbite treatment, and they'd be wishing they'd sewn those dust ruffles themselves. Even if she'd wanted them in a bunny and ducky print.

CHAPTER SIX

Faith headed over to the assembly hall that afternoon alone. Everyone else was walking in clusters of twos and threes. *They* had friends because *they* knew how to behave themselves with other people. *They* didn't get their hackles up and alienate the first two people they met at school.

Shelley probably hated her for life, and with pretty good reason. What had the poor girl done, really, that was so awful? So she acted a little surprised that her new roommate was black. Where Shelley came from, a black person was probably a rarity. Faith could see now that she might have been a little more understanding about this — instead of responding as though Shelley had said she thought they ought to reinstate slavery. Now it was probably too late to undo all the harm that had been done.

The harm now also included her start at a friendship with Dana. After Shelley had flown out of the room in humiliation, Dana said she was getting out for a while, too.

"I'm going to walk into Greenleaf and see what's happening there. I'm getting depressed here. Nobody in this room seems to be able to get along for more than five minutes."

"You act like it's totally my fault," Faith said. "I didn't hear you *oohing* and *ahhing* over her decorating ideas."

"Well, I don't want doilies on the desk chairs, that's for sure. I couldn't think of a way to tell her that right off, but I think we could have talked her out of most of her ideas without insulting her. It just went so stupidly. She was only trying to be friendly. I can see that now, and what did we do? We froze her out. Oh, Faith, I'm getting tired of all this trouble over everything. What *did* she do to you that was so awful? How did all this get started?"

Faith felt backed into a corner. She didn't want to admit she might have jumped to conclusions, so she said, "I just get the feeling she's not crazy about my color."

"Faith, I don't think she knows enough about blacks to know if she likes them or not." And with that she was gone.

Faith waited around the room for them to come back before the headmistress's welcome address at two. When no one had showed up by five to two, Faith gave up and walked across the campus green by herself.

The assembly hall was practically full by the time Faith got there. Although she knew Dana and Shelley were there, she couldn't see either of them in the crowd. She spotted a cluster of empty seats way in the back, off to the side. She took a seat in the middle of that section. As long as she was going to be a loner, she might as well play the part.

At precisely two o'clock, Patrice Allardyce, the headmistress, came out from behind the curtain at the left side of the stage and walked over to the podium. She was extremely sophisticated-looking — tall and blond, with her hair pulled up in a French twist. She was wearing a silk suit in a natural color with a soft brown cotton shirt underneath. She was very good-looking, but in a frosty way. Faith had heard that around here she was respected but also feared.

Patrice Allardyce didn't read from any

notes. She just stood for maybe a full minute, staring openly at the assembled crowd
of girls, as if sizing them up. Then she
smiled an icy smile and began.

"Good afternoon, girls. I am Patrice Allardyce, headmistress of Canby Hall. I'm de-
lighted to see you all managed to arrive here
on time. Punctuality is one of the basics of
good manners expected of Canby girls."

As she spoke these words, a single unman-
nerly, unpunctual Canby girl lurched into
the hall. She got halfway down the aisle, saw
there were no seats, looked back and saw
the empty section where Faith was sitting,
ran back up to it, climbed over a half-dozen
girls, and slumped into the seat next to
Faith's. During this whole time, Patrice Allardyce stood silently watching.

"Of course," she went on after the girl was
seated, "some Canby girls are more unwill-
ing learners than others. There are even a
few who haven't learned proper conduct after an entire year here. I wonder if you could
stop by my office after the assembly, Miss
Flint, so we can discuss the problems you
seem to be having with your overcrowded
schedule, or whatever it is that's forcing you
to be late for important commitments."

As she spoke, Patrice Allardyce was look-

ing directly at the girl who had sat down
next to Faith. When she was finished, the
girl replied, under her breath, "Okay, P.A.
I'll stop by for a little visit. Sorry I was late.
I was in the middle of an important nap,
which I'll get back to as soon as you get rolling again."

Then she turned slightly toward Faith
and said, "P.A.'s speeches are the best sleep
aids since Nytol."

Faith looked over. The girl was small with
short, curly blond hair and a sprinkling of
freckles across her nose — tomboyish and
clearly full of fun. Faith liked her instantly.

Patrice Allardyce started her talk again,
first singing the praises of Canby Hall and
its great tradition, emphasizing the good
fortune of every girl here to be part of this
tradition.

She told the story of Canby Hall.

"Canby Hall was founded in 1897 when
Julia Canby, the only child of Horace Canby,
a wealthy industrialist, died of fever while
abroad in Europe. In tribute to her, he estab-
lished a girls' school on the property that
would have been her inheritance.

"The family home, facing the long oblong
park with its wishing pool, became the home
of the school's headmistress. Many have

lived there before me. Each has left something of her style, her taste, behind in that house.

"The chapel, the farm and stables, and Julia's skating pond have been maintained as they were in Julia's time.

"The school opened with just thirty girls. Main Building and Baker House were the first buildings on campus. A portrait of Julia Canby at age thirteen hangs in the reception room of Main. As the school grew, Addison House and Charles House were built and an addition was made to Main Building. The Esther Watkins Library, the bequest of an early student, was built later, as was the Science Building, the gift of various alumnae.

"Many features of the original estate bring the same pleasure to the girls of Canby Hall today that they brought to Julia Canby — the skating pond, the wooded paths and picnic areas, the summer house by my residence. The wishing pond in the park is still stocked with golden carp. The statue of the lioness with cubs in the birch grove was the gift of the Class of 1917 on the twentieth anniversary of the school's founding.

"In accordance with Horace Canby's requests, experiences of traditional New England activities are included in the school calendar. In autumn, apple butter from the orchard's harvest is cooked outdoors in antique black pots, to be enjoyed with homemade bread made by the girls, along with fresh butter from the school farm. In the spring, the maple trees of the north grove are tapped. The boiling down of the syrup ends with a pancake festival to which both parents and alumnae are invited, along with the students."

"If she goes on much longer with this kind of stuff," the girl next to Faith said, "I'm going to die of terminal quaintness."

Patrice Allardyce didn't hear this, of course, so she kept on going with her speech.

"Of course," she said, "with tradition comes the responsibility of upholding it. Academic excellence is part of this tradition, as is ladylike behavior. A strict adherence to the principles of the school is expected of all Canby Hall girls."

Faith wasn't sure what these principles were specifically, but was pretty sure they didn't say fool around all you want.

Then Patrice Allardyce moved through the areas of trouble a Canby Hall girl should avoid.

"On the issue of boys," she was saying,

"your handbook covers the subject in detail, so I'll just highlight. They are welcome on campus only during nonclass, nonstudy hours, and on weekends. They may be entertained outdoors, or in the reception areas of the dormitory residences, or in student quarters during specified open houses. It should go without saying that proper conduct is expected of Canby girls in all social situations, and that public displays of affection are not acceptable social behavior, with the exception of discreet hand-holding."

The girl whispered to Faith, "Now you've got to ask yourself what that means — *discreet* hand-holding. With gloves on? Until your palms get sweaty? That's probably it. I'll bet P.A.'s mind curdles at the thought of a Canby girl's palm sweating in the grip of an Oakley Prep boy."

"Drinking," Patrice was saying now, "is strictly against school rules. But it shouldn't be even a consideration — rules or no rules — for the true Canby girl. The true Canby girl knows that when you're drinking, you're not really having fun, you just *think* you're having fun."

"Boy," Faith said to the girl, getting into the heckling spirit, "that's really splitting hairs."

Between the two of them, Faith and the
girl kept a whispered running commentary
going through the rest of Patrice Allardyce's
speech. They thought they were terrifically
funny. Patrice Allardyce did not. A couple
of times she glanced over in their direction
and noted that they were whispering, even
though she couldn't hear what they were
saying. Faith knew right away that being
friends with this girl could be dangerous,
but she did like her attitude. Faith wanted to
do well here, but she didn't figure that re-
quired getting all sappy about Canby Hall.
If she was going to get through these years,
it wouldn't hurt to have someone around
with a sense of humor.

She and the girl, Casey Flint, introduced
themselves to each other after the address.
Casey was a sophomore, too, but this was
her second year at Canby.

"I'm barely here this year," she said, running her fingers through her hair. "I got in a
little trouble during spring term and nearly
got thrown out. But I begged P.A. for mercy,
threw myself at her feet."

"You didn't," Faith said. She had trouble
imagining Casey begging anyone for mercy.

"Practically," Casey said. "I really don't
want to get thrown out of here. It's the best

of the three schools my folks have shipped
me off to. And the one they've got lined up
in case I get tossed out of here is one of those
semi-prisons for problem kids. I mean I think
they tie you in your bed at night. This place
isn't all that bad, really. P.A.'s the worst of
it. Most of the teachers and houseparents
are okay. Where are you living?"

"Baker," Faith said.

"Oh. Me, too. We've got Alison Cavanaugh
for housemother. She's terrific. Very hip.
Hey, being in the same house, we can eat
together. Want to go down to dinner with me
tonight?"

Faith, who had been sure she'd have to
eat alone, said yes without a second's
hesitation.

She had a great time with Casey and some
of her friends at dinner, laughing so hard
tears rolled down her cheeks. She completely
forgot, for an hour, about the situation in
her room. And so, she was taken aback when
she came in to find that major rearranging
had taken place. There was now a bed and
desk in each of three corners. White adhe-
sive tape ran from the ceiling down the walls
and across the floor, dividing the room into
quarters — three living sections and an

empty one marked with a sign taped to the floor: FREE SPACE/WALK-THROUGH.

Both Dana and Shelley were there when Faith came through the door. Shelley didn't look up. She was writing another letter. Dana was stretched out on her bed, reading a novel. She gave Faith a look that was questioning. Then she went back to reading, as if to confirm that all communications here had been shut down.

Faith turned and noticed that another sign had been taped to the back of the door. It read:

SHELLEY'S FINAL DECORATING IDEA

Things went on like this for a week. The three of them started classes. Dana tried out for the choir. Faith went over to the school paper to see if she could get a photo assignment. They all began to get to know girls in their classes, on the floor. Faith spent a lot of time with Casey Flint. School life at Canby Hall was grinding into gear and they were a part of it — but separately. When they came back to their room, the rule of silence and isolation held firm, even grew stronger as each of them became determined not to be the first to give in.

The tape stayed up. Everyone was careful not to stray over anyone else's line. The only communication was by note, usually sarcastic.

"Do you think you could possibly turn your radio down a little so other people could study?" Shelley wrote to Faith.

"I'd appreciate it if people would not leave opened sardine cans on the radiator. I'd rather not live in some place that smells like a fishing dock." Dana passed a copy of this to each of them, since she didn't know whom the sardines belonged to.

Everybody in the dorm knew not to come into the room to visit. Word got around fast that it was an armed camp. But apparently the word didn't get as far as Alison Cavanaugh, the housemother, because when she stopped by the following Sunday night, it was clear she was startled by what she saw.

"Hi!" she said as she came into the room. "This is my first round of room visits. I just wanted to see how everything's going for you around here."

It wasn't until she was through with this little speech that she took in what was going on. When she did, it stopped her dead in her tracks.

"Oh, my. I see we've got a trouble spot here."

All three girls just stared at her. No one wanted to do the explaining.

"Don't all talk at once," Alison said.

"It just didn't work out with us," Dana finally said.

"I think we'd better have a talk about this." Alison looked at the girls hopefully.

"There's nothing to talk about," Shelley answered quickly.

"Oh, it looks to me like there's quite a bit to talk about. I want you all up in my apartment in an hour. That'll give me time to work up a little tea and cookies. That makes this sound like a social invitation, but it isn't. I won't have trouble spots in my house. I've got my reputation to think about. So we're going to do whatever it takes to sort this out."

"I don't think I can make it," Shelley said.

Alison pretended she hadn't heard this.

"It's now" — she looked at her digital watch — "six-seventeen. I want you at my door at seven-thirty."

With that, she turned and walked out.

CHAPTER
SEVEN

Dana fell in love at first sight with Alison's apartment. It was exactly the kind of place she imagined living in when she was grown-up and an independent career woman.

It was up in the attic of Baker. Outside of the room was a huge bulletin board filled with notices the girls might be interested in. A weekend sign-out sheet was right in the middle. Alison's room looked nothing like the rest of the dorm. It had been Alison-ized. Posters from art exhibits filled one wall of the living room. The only thing on the facing wall was a neon sign from an old beauty shop. It was a crossed scissors and comb with letters underneath spelling out, KATIE'S KLIP 'N' KURL.

There were plumbing pipes and heating ducts running along the ceiling, but instead of trying to hide or ignore them, Alison had made them part of the decor by painting them in bright, primary, high-gloss colors — red, blue, yellow, green.

Alison herself was a lot like her apartment — stylish, warm, open. Her appearance was a dramatic one. No one would miss her in a crowd. She had a wild mass of wavy reddish-brown hair. She wore large horn-rimmed glasses that were always slipping down her nose and constantly being pushed back up again with an index finger. Alison was almost always in mid-gesture. She used her hands as much as her mouth when she talked. She had an aura of energy. She gave the impression that she was always racing, that the one life she'd been given wasn't going to be nearly enough time to get everything done, that now that she was in her late twenties she had no time to waste.

When the girls came in, Alison told them to just flop anywhere while she got the tea tray. There were three comfortable armchairs and a wild scattering of floor pillows. The three of them sat down on these, as far apart from each other as the room would allow. No one said a word during the few minutes it took Alison to return. They stared at the bookcases lining one wall and the coffee table filled with magazines.

Alison came back with an ancient, beat-up Coca-Cola tray loaded down with a steaming teapot, mugs, a sugar box, a carton of milk, two bags of cookies, and a ham sandwich.

"The sandwich is my dinner. I didn't get down to the dining hall in time tonight. So. You can be my dinner companions. Keep that in mind while you tell me this story of yours. Try not to give me ulcers."

Nobody responded to this overture. They sat silently. They didn't take anything from the tea tray.

"Come on," Alison encouraged them. "You've each got to have at least one cookie and a cup of tea. If I'm the only one eating, I'll get self-conscious. I'll worry that you're all listening to me chew."

And so they each dutifully took a cup and a cookie and sank back onto their pillows in silence.

"Hey," Alison said. "I don't expect this'll be easy, but I want you to try. I think the best way would be to go around in a circle, starting with" — she pointed at Dana, who was to her immediate left — "and just tell me your side of what's been going on since you got here. Don't hold back. What we're going for here is truth, not politeness."

She looked hard at Dana to prompt her.

"Well," Dana said, "I'm probably not the one to be doing the real talking. It's mostly their fight. I'd like us to all get along. And I think we could, if they'd just ease off. I think things just got off on the wrong foot, and no one can get it back on the right one now without losing face. I wish we could, though."

"But what's the issue here?" Alison asked. "Where did the problem start? Why don't you fill me in from your side, Shelley?"

"She's mean to me," Shelley said, nodding toward Faith without looking at her. "Every time I try to be friendly, she snaps my head off. I think I said something in the beginning that made her think I was put off by her being black. But honestly, I'm not. It's just something new to me, having a black friend. I think she took my surprise for horror or something. And now she hates me. Well, let her. She thinks — actually they both do — that they're so cool just because they're from big cities. And they've decided I'm a hick, standing in a pasture with straw in my teeth, saying 'yup' and 'nope.' Even if we get this problem settled, I don't think they're ever going to like me. Even if I say I'm sorry — which I am — that I unintention-ally offended her, they're still probably going to make remarks about me and laugh behind my back. Well, let them. I don't care. I don't care about anything at this stupid school. I never wanted to come here in the first place, and now I just want to go home more than ever."

During the last part of this little speech, Shelley had begun to cry. Not sobs, just a steady stream of tears down her round cheeks. Dana pulled a few paper napkins off the pile on the tray and handed them to Shelley.

"Hey," Dana said. "I can't speak for any-one else, but I never meant to make you feel I thought you were a hick. And I've never laughed behind your back. I think it's sort of neat that you're from someplace not like my place. Meeting different kinds of people is part of what I came here for."

Shelley looked up at her as if she wanted to believe her but wasn't sure.

"Honest," Dana reassured her.

Shelley smiled the faintest beginning of a smile.

"I guess," Alison said, "yours is the only side left to hear, Faith."

"I don't know," Faith said, looking at Shelley. "I don't remember what I thought of you before I got mad. I know you're different from me because you're from a small town, but I don't think different means worse. I just didn't like the way you came in, looking at me like I was a porpoise at the Seaquarium. I thought I'd give you the fisheye right back. Then by the time I realized that you probably hadn't meant to be insulting, we were too far gone into this. I just haven't been able to see a way out of it."

"You could have told each other all this," Alison said.

"Well, I guess I just did," Faith said and smiled a little. "It was easier than I thought." She looked back at Shelley and went on. "I'd like to start over, Shelley. I think it'd be a good thing for us to try to be friends. It'd be dumb to try to say we aren't very different. We've spent the past fifteen years living completely different lives. Like when your family was having Christmas turkey, mine was in the ghetto frying up the neighborhood pigeon."

"No!" Shelley gasped.

Faith broke into a grin. "If you believed

that one, maybe there *isn't* much hope for us."

Dana held her breath. If Shelley took offense here, they were back to square one. Shelley didn't say anything for a long moment, then she said to Faith, "Okay. I might've believed the pigeon story for a second, but I'll bet if I told you I had a pet pig back home named Sylvester, you wouldn't be one-hundred percent sure if I was lying or not."

Faith thought for a minute, then smiled and said, "You're right. You've got me there, girl."

Both of them laughed at this, and then the laughter spread. Dana caught it, then Alison, who said, "Hey. I think maybe we did it. Did we?"

All three girls looked first at each other, then at Alison, and nodded happily.

"Shake on it?" Alison said.

They leaned in off their pillows and held hands in a circle for a minute.

"Well, I guess I've earned my keep tonight," Alison said. "And you can earn yours by taking the wreckage from this tea party out to the kitchen and cleaning up. I've got to go check out a rumor about a cocker spaniel someone's supposedly hiding in one of the rooms."

Dana, Faith, and Shelley all started to laugh again. Alison threw up her hands.

"You laugh, but this is my life. Really, there are moments, poking under beds for hidden pets is a good example, when I think maybe I should've gone into aeronautical engineering or orthodontics, instead of housemothering."

Then she was gone in a flash, leaving the three girls alone. They sat there for a minute, and Dana finally spoke.

"Do you think we could just start over — pretend it's the first day and just start from scratch?"

"I don't think we have to do that," Faith said, crossing her legs yoga-style, grabbing the toes of her shoes. "I think we've come through a hard time to a better place. We've learned a lot about each other through the fight, like . . . you know, each other's sensitive areas."

"We know Dana hates sardines," Shelley said shyly.

Everybody laughed, then got serious again.

"Anyway," Faith went on, "I think we could use this stuff we know about each

other positively — to be more understanding."

"And if anything goes wrong," Dana said,
taking a cookie off the platter, "I think we
ought to talk right away — not let things
build up again, ever."

"And I don't care if we ever decorate,"
Shelley said. "I don't care if the place looks
like the black hole of Calcutta. Oh, no!" She
put her hand over her mouth. "That isn't
about something black, is it? I didn't just put
my foot in it again, did I?"

The other two laughed.

"No," Faith said. "I think the black hole
is just dark inside. You can talk about Black
Beauty, too. And blackboards. I'll give you
a list."

"Hey," Dana said, getting up off the floor,
"what do you say we get this mess cleaned
up so we can get back up to the black hole —
our black hole?"

CHAPTER EIGHT

Dear Paul (Honeybear),

Well, the war in Room 407 is over. I'm now living with two friends instead of two enemies — thanks to Alison Cavanaugh, World's Greatest Housemother. She got us to talk out our problems and clear the air, and it worked! I think Dana and Faith still think I'm different, but okay different, not weird different. And since the powwow, we've really been getting to be good friends.

They really work hard at cheering me up, but I'm still sad most of the time, wanting to be back there in Pine Bluff. Hoping that, come Christmas, I will be back there for good keeps me from wanting to get into anything here. Like, I was thinking about trying out for the swim team, but then I thought, why bother? Most of the big meets are after the holidays when, with luck, I won't be here. So it would probably mean practicing for nothing.

There's a lot of social life here, stuff with the boys from Oakley down the road. But I'm not interested in them either. I've already got the best boyfriend in the world, so why would I want to meet anyone else? I guess you probably feel the same way back there.

They give us bunches of homework here. I have to put in a lot of time to keep up. Some of the classes are a lot like at Polk. French is still a lot of memorizing, which I'm awful at. For English, though, I'm taking a course in modern American writers, which is fun. And for history, I've got an independent study, which means no classes. I just read on my own — my subject is the Phoenicians — and then talk with my history advisor once a week.

Other stuff here is not so neat. The food, for instance. Most of the time, you don't even want to know what they're serving in the hot line. Usually, I just head for the salad bar, but I'm beginning to be afraid I'm going to turn into a rabbit from all the lettuce I'm eating (ha ha). I guess it's good for my *weight, though. Now, if Mom would just stop sending cookies and other goodies, I could probably be a shadow of my former self by the time I get back there.*

Your first letter was wonderful. I nearly died waiting for it. I was beginning to think they'd closed down the Pine Bluff P.O. Ted's party does sound like it was a lot of fun. I can just picture you all singing around the campfire at midnight in the moonlight. Just don't have too much fun, though, without

Your loving
Shelley
(Honeybunch)

CHAPTER
NINE

By Friday afternoon of the second week of classes, Faith was exhausted. The public school she'd gone to in D.C. was good, but she'd come to Canby Hall because it was supposed to be better. For some reason, she hadn't made the connection between better and tougher. And Canby Hall was tough! You could get tired just carrying around all the books the teachers assigned, let alone reading them.

Plus, she'd gone over on Wednesday to the office of the school newspaper — the *Canby Clarion* — with a portfolio of her top photos. The best she'd hoped for was that they'd consider her for some future assignment. But it turned out that two of their staff photographers had transferred out over the summer. They were drastically short-handed and gave Faith an assignment right on the spot.

Since Wednesday she had been spending every spare minute going around with one of the *Clarion* reporters, doing a photo feature about incoming freshmen, with quotes on their first impressions of Canby Hall. They wanted to run a picture for each girl. She had just taken, developed, and printed the last two that afternoon after classes. By the time she got back to Baker, all she wanted to do with the weekend was sleep through it.

407 had really changed from the bare room they had moved into. Not that they had followed through on Shelley's idea of decorating. What happened instead was that they had just sort of started filling in blanks here and there. The walls were covered, from big things, like Faith's Humphrey Bogart poster and Dana's Joffrey Ballet poster, to tiny things, like Shelley's snapshots from home and Faith's graffiti photos. She liked to take pictures of wall scribblings. Lots of these were jokes, such as "What's soft and white and *very* dangerous? — Shark-infested custard." They had also put up tiny nails

and hung all their scarves and beads and hats on them to make a sort of free-form wall-hanging.

Like almost everybody in Baker, they had put their bed frames in the storage room, set their mattresses on the floor, and covered them with as many blankets and quilts as they had, to make floating island couches out of them.

On the windowsill, they had made an arrangement of coffee mugs stuffed with dried flowers, jars filled with colored Magic Markers and pencils, and Shelley's piggy bank.

They really liked the atmosphere they had created. They were all pretty accepting of each other's things and were about the same degree of neat — midway between really neat and total slobs.

Dana and Shelley were waiting up in the room for her, so they could all go down to dinner together. Faith came through the door to find them sprawled facedown on their beds, as if they were dead. There was a copy of one of last term's *Clarion*s propped up on Faith's desk. Over the real headline they had taped one they'd done in Magic Marker. It read:

Two Students Starve
Waiting for Roommate:
said she'd be back by five

Faith exploded with laughter and ran over to shake and tickle the dead back to life.

"Okay, okay, you two," she said. "I'm sorry. Someone was hogging the darkroom, and I had to cool my heels for an hour before I could get in and print my stuff. Tell you what. We can go into Greenleaf after dinner, and I'll treat to cones at the ice cream place."

Dana sat up in bed. "Did you forget? Tonight's the mixer — you know, the record hop — at Oakley. They say the first one of the term is always the biggest and best. Everybody goes."

"Well, it'll have to be everybody minus one," Faith said, and yawned. "I'm way too beat to boogie tonight."

"Make that everybody minus two," Shelley said, reaching down behind her bed for her knitting bag with the pink sweater she was working on in it. "I wrote Paul that I'd call him tonight."

"So?" Dana said. "You can go to the mixer and call him later."

"No. I want to think about the call first, for a while. You know — what I'm going to say. What he'll say."

"Why don't you two just mail each other scripts then?" Faith asked. "Save the long distance bucks."

Shelley stuck her tongue out at Faith.

"Hardhearted Faith," she said. "You don't know a think about love, I bet. You've never been in love, have you?"

"Nope," Faith said smugly. "But when I am, I can tell you I won't be mushy about it. I'll be just as practical as I am about everything else. It's just the way I am."

"We'll see," Shelley said, sounding like a fortune-teller.

Faith was glad Shelley was taking the teasing good-naturedly, which was how it was intended. But deep inside, she really did think Shelley was kind of a drip about Paul. She knew that if she ever did fall in love, she *was* going to be a little cooler about it. She'd make a point not to hang around, going endlessly through snapshots of the guy. She'd restrain herself from reading his letters aloud to her friends — especially if the best parts were how he had really missed her at the football pep rally, and missed how her voice squeaked with excitement on the cheers. As far as Faith was concerned, Paul sounded like the dullest guy in the world.

Well, next to her Uncle Felix, who never said anything at family dinners except "Pass the potatoes." But she wouldn't think of letting Shelley see that she felt this way. She listened to the details of the romance as if they were Romeo and Juliet. She figured that's what friends were for.

After dinner, going for an ice cream cone still sounded like a good idea to Faith. Plus it sounded like a manageable amount of activity for the night. Going straight to bed after supper on a Friday night, seemed just too depressing for a fifteen-year-old, and she could probably stay awake through a double-dip.

Since neither Dana nor Shelley were interested, and since she didn't want to go alone, she called Casey on the inter-dorm phone in the room.

"Hey, you going to the mixer or what?" she asked Casey when she got her on the line.

"Are you kidding? I went to one of those last year. Have you gotten a look at the guys from Oakley yet? About the only fun you can have at a mixer there is looking at them line the wall in the gym. You can play Count the Zits."

"That bad?" Faith said, not believing it.

"My dear, we are talking about major gross-out," Casey said vehemently. "Are you going?"

"No. I'm beat. I thought I'd go into town and get an ice cream." Faith twisted the phone cord, waiting.

"Well, have fun," Casey said.

With anyone else, Faith would think that this meant she didn't want to go, but this was Casey Flint she was talking to. Casey was determinedly difficult. It was part of her general I-don't-care attitude, to show as little interest in everything as possible.

"So," Faith pushed a little, "you want to go?"

"Sure. See you in the lounge in five minutes," Casey answered without hesitating.

On the front of the door to every room in Baker was a sign-out sheet. Before a Canby Hall girl could leave the campus she had to fill in the time she was leaving, when she expected to be back, and when she returned, the time she had come in. Faith scribbled in seven-thirty and nine-thirty and ran down to the lounge on the first floor.

They walked the mile into town. It was that part of the fall when the days had an overlay of warmth, but as soon as the sun went down, the bottom dropped out, and it was pretty cold.

"Land sakes!" Faith said, zipping up her windbreaker. "We should've worn mittens. It's really frosty up in this here neck of the woods."

"Yup," Casey said, "shur is."

They liked to do this, pretend they were rural New Englanders. Casey was from Manhattan. Her parents were very rich — big-time art dealers. You'd never know it to look at her, though. She wore jeans as much as school rules would allow, never flaunted her spending money, and never mentioned her family. Faith only found out about them through the gossip mill, which cranked nonstop at Canby Hall, night and day. But there was a lot she still didn't know about Casey's background, and thought she'd try asking a few questions.

"Your folks coming up for parents' weekend?"

"No way," Casey said, putting on her tough voice. "I think they might be coming up for my graduation. Remind me to let them know about that at Christmas. That'll give them a couple of years' advance notice."

"I gather you don't see them much," Faith said hesitantly.

"Once in a while. They send me photos of themselves every now and then, so I'll be able to recognize them when they pick me up at the train station. They're out of the country a lot. Spain and Italy mostly. They buy and sell sculptures, which strikes me as an incredibly boring way to make a living. Most of the stuff they buy looks to me as if it was done by monkeys."

"How do you feel about them?" Faith asked.

"They don't give me much to feel good about. Last year they mailed my birthday present to the school I went to before Canby. They *forgot* where I was, as if I was a hat or something. I mean — well, let me put it this way — if they had a TV game show where you could win a new set of parents, I'd try like crazy to get on it. I'd ask for some like Shelley's. You know, a real mommy-mom who bakes chocolate chip cookies and a dad who falls asleep every night in his chair in front of the TV. I wouldn't even care if they were old fuddy-duddies or put real strict rules on me. Just so they were there." A slight tremor had crept into her voice as she talked. It was even more noticeable when she said, "A lot of the time, I feel way too alone. I get scared, and there's no one to turn to." She stopped abruptly, as if wary of revealing too much of herself.

They had gotten to town and walked across the main street to Tutti-Frutti, the ice cream place. Although Greenleaf was a small town out in the country, it was loaded with tourists in the summer and students the rest of the year, so it was full of shops with funky names. The Tutti-Frutti was decked out like an Italian café, with white and dark green walls and white Formica tables. Casey called it the Tutti Muchi.

"You want to have a sundae instead of a cone?" Faith asked. "I'm starving. I couldn't eat whatever that was at dinner tonight."

"Poached eggs with cream sauce on toast," Casey said. "Everybody calls it Dead Men on a Raft. Sure. I could go for a hot fudge. Besides, if we have a sundae, we can get a table and hang out for a while."

They got a booth in the back and ordered two *Ciao Bambinos*, which was what the menu called hot fudge sundaes. Faith ordered an extra scoop. She always thought she could eat all the ice cream in the world, then, halfway through a sundae, got so full she began to think she would never be able to eat another bite of ice cream in her life.

"What about yours?" Casey asked as she pulled the cherry off the top of her sundae and held it by the stem in midair, about to drop it into her mouth.

"My what?" Faith asked.

"Your *family*. I mean, I know the basic outline, but I'm interested in the details. Not to mention my curiosity about life among the Negroes."

Faith would've decked anyone else for this remark, but she knew Casey was being sarcastic, so Faith responded in the same tone.

"Oh, you know. It's chicken and watermelon every night. And then we put on our pink satin tuxedos and play soul records." Faith kept a straight face.

"Do you ever worry," Casey said, suddenly serious, "that some people you meet really think that sort of stuff?"

"Sure. Some probably do, but usually it's more hidden. Around here, with a lot of the white girls, I can tell that first off I'm black, then me. They see the color before they see the person."

"I guess it's that way when you're in any minority," Casey said thoughtfully. "I had a friend at the last school I went to. She was a knockout. I thought she was so lucky. I used to fantasize what it'd be like being so beautiful that when I walked into a party, everything would just sort of stop for a minute. Then I got to know her better and found out she was always worried that people only liked her for her looks, that they didn't care what she was like underneath. It's a little like that being rich."

"You think everyone likes you for your money?" Faith asked with surprise.

"No. I mean it's not as though I'm buying them fur coats. *Then* they might like me for my money. They just think I'm different because of it. They think I'm spoiled or a snob. They just stick their label on me." The way Casey said this clearly indicated that it hurt her a lot.

"Yeah. Same with me. But you know what?" Faith said, and smiled.

"What?"

"Even if it's hard sometimes, there's nobody I'd rather be than me," Faith said firmly.

"Ditto," Casey said. "Ditto for sure. In fact,

I guess I really *like* being a little different from everybody else. I know I wouldn't like to be one of those girls who work so hard at being *just* like everyone else. They're careful to use only this month's expressions, this year's shade of lipstick. The insiders."

"We should start a club," Faith said. "The Outsiders."

"Who'd belong?" Casey asked.

"Just us."

"Not a bad idea," Casey said, and smiled. She had a great one. When she smiled, her whole being grinned. "We wouldn't have to worry about renting big halls for our meetings."

"We wouldn't have to spend a lot of energy on membership drives," Faith added.

"What about dues?" Casey said.

"I'll buy the sundaes at this meeting. You get them the next time." Faith held out her hand.

"You've sold me. I'll join," Casey said, shaking Faith's hand.

Faith yawned. "Oh, oh," she said. "I guess I'm fading fast. You'd better get me out of here before I fall asleep and you have to carry me back to campus."

"Oh, darn," Casey said, laughing. "I guess that means we'll have to wait until next time to work out the secret handshake and blood initiation."

CHAPTER TEN

Almost everybody, at least everybody in Baker, *did* go to the mixer. Shelley listened to them leave in twos and threes and fours, laughing out of nervousness and anticipation because anything could happen at a mixer — or nothing.

Shelley knew what they were feeling but couldn't feel it herself. She was never going to be a part of what was going on here. Not really. Not when everything and everybody she loved was a thousand miles away.

She missed her family terribly. Her mom had sent her a tin of her terrific caramel corn this week, but every time Shelley opened the can, the smell made her so nostalgic for home that she had started to cry.

The third time she did this, Faith took the can away from her.

"You're just going to get it all soggy. Dana and I have no sentimental attachment at all to this corn, so we'll be able to put it to its proper use — being eaten."

When the last of the rush to leave had quieted down, the dorm was silent except for the dim sounds of the distant radio of some other lonely girl down the hall. Shelley thought a little music might help her, too. She got out all her favorite albums and played them one by one. Listening to them sort of depressed her, but also made her feel closer to home.

Then she got out her Japanese paper folder — the one she used to hold all her favorite snapshots. She looked at them one by one. In the back was the packet of pictures of Paul.

There was one cut out of the school paper, showing him spiking a football in the end zone, looking scruffed up and totally cute in his jersey. In the photo taken at the beach last summer, Paul was lifting her out of the water. He was tan, the ends of his hair blond.

There was one with him astride a tractor

on his dad's farm, shirtless in a cowboy hat.
This one was her favorite.

There were more, but she couldn't go on.
It hurt too much.

She looked at the clock. It was only nine.
Two more hours until the rates changed and
she could call. How was she going to wait
that long? She wondered if anyone had ever
died of waiting, just had a heart attack or
something.

She got out her French book and tried to
study, but it didn't have the power to hold
her attention — French never did. It was
her worst subject. In class, she often drifted
into the clouds. She'd been caught a couple
of times. Mr. Washburn knew she was lost
in space. She'd had a terrible moment with
him during Thursday's class.

"Où est la bibliothèque?" he asked. "Made-
moiselle Hyde?"

Panic. She knew he'd asked one of the
study questions, but she hadn't the vaguest
idea which one. She tried to bluff.

"Oui. Je vais faire un pique-nique."

"Oh?" he said. "So you're going to have a
picnic in the library? I don't think they go
for that around here. It brings the ants
inside."

The whole class cracked up. She turned beet red.

On Friday, he had given her a hard time, calling on her more often than on the other girls, just to make sure she was paying attention. She knew he thought she was a bubblehead. He didn't realize she was a tragic figure.

This was how she saw herself, like the heroines of the romantic novels she read. A girl desperate in the agony of being so cruelly separated from the ones she loved; driven away from her home; forced to live away at a boarding school, like Jane Eyre.

Not that Canby Hall was such a bad place. Actually, it was a lot better than she had expected. It just wasn't where she wanted to be.

She had thought of deliberately flunking out. It would be easy enough, given how little interest she had in her classes, but her pride wouldn't let her. So, she'd have to get herself out the hard way, with a steady stream of letters to her parents detailing her misery. Then she'd talk with them over Christmas break, tug their heartstrings, and make them see that they simply had to let her stay in Pine Bluff.

She fell asleep during this fantasy —

which ended with her parents nodding in unison, filled with understanding of her feelings, and happy that she was going to be back home with them where she belonged.

She woke to find it was eleven-thirty, half an hour past the time she and Paul had arranged that she'd call! She grabbed her change purse, flew down the hall to the stairwell, and raced to the main floor where the pay phones were. She couldn't believe it — two other girls were already using them. Both were deep in what were clearly romantic conversations of their own. Who knew how long they'd be on?

She was in her robe, so she couldn't make a fast dash over to Addison or Charles. She had to first run up to the room, put on jeans and a sweater, and run down again. She got to the first floor and realized she'd left the change purse on the bed. This was beginning to be like one of those nervous nightmares she sometimes had. Finally, she got it all together and lurched across the lawn to Addison, where — mercifully — there was no one on either phone. Absolute privacy! Bliss!

She dialed Paul's area code and number and put in her money after the operator told her the amount. She worried about calling so late. By now it was almost a quarter to twelve. He was probably frantic by now.

The phone rang once, twice, three times. Odd. She would've thought he'd be sitting on top of it. On the fourth ring, someone picked up.

Hello?"

It was Paul's mother. Her groggy voice clearly indicated that *she* had not been sitting on top of the phone but had been sound asleep.

Shelley almost hung up at this point from lack of nerve, but changed her mind. If she hung up, it might frighten poor Mrs. Clifford. She might think it was a creepy caller. So Shelley said, as brightly as possible, "Hi, Mrs. Clifford. Is Paul there?"

"Who is this?"

"It's Shelley."

"Aren't you supposed to be at school?" Mrs. Clifford yawned.

"I *am* at school. I told Paul I'd call tonight. I fell asleep, though, and missed the time we'd planned. I hope he isn't frantic." Shelley felt embarrassed and foolish.

"I don't think so. I don't think he's even here," Mrs. Clifford said sleepily.

"He must be there. He probably came in while you were asleep. Could you just check his room for me?" Shelley's voice rose with nervousness.

"Okay," Mrs. Clifford said, ending with a heavy sigh to show she thought this was a lot for Shelley to ask and totally useless.

Shelley waited on the line for what seemed like two hours but was probably only two minutes, until Paul's mother came back.

"No. He's not here. Tonight was the 4-H hayride. They were going all the way out to Boone's Woods for it, I think. When he left, Paul said he and a bunch of the boys would just camp out there and come back in the morning. Is something wrong? I mean is this an emergency?"

"No," Shelley said. "It's nothing important."

"Well, I'll leave a message that you called. I'm sure he'll get back to you," Mrs. Clifford said with finality.

Shelley could almost hear Mrs. Clifford's smug satisfaction. She liked Shelley well enough, but thought she took up too much of Paul's attention and time. Like Shelley's parents, she thought the couple was too serious for college-bound teenagers with years of school ahead of them.

"Well, thanks, Mrs. Clifford. Sorry to have

bothered you. I didn't mean to wake anybody up," Shelley said apologetically.

"It's okay, Michelle. I hope you're enjoying that new school of yours."

"Oh, sure. It's terrific." Shelley sat numbly holding the receiver for a minute before finally hanging it up.

Just terrific. Everything was terrific. She hated it here, had been enduring it all week just by looking forward to this moment, and what a moment it had turned out to be. Here she was, gone barely two weeks and already she was fading from Paul's mind. How *could* he forget their phone call? She'd been waiting for it for seven straight days. If she hadn't spoken to his mother and found out about the hayride, she would've thought that he was dead. Death was the only thing that could have made *her* miss the call. She couldn't believe he didn't feel the same way. She didn't know what to think. She felt like her whole world was collapsing around her.

She shuffled slowly up the stairs to the room. Faith was sound asleep. She had come back from town while Shelley had been playing records earlier and had gone straight to bed. Thankfully, Faith could sleep through a tornado, so she never minded anyone's noise.

While Shelley had been on the phone, Dana had come back from the mixer, and she was still up. In fact, she was the most up Shelley had ever seen. She was sitting on her bed, looking off into the distance, a really dopey smile on her face, her eyes bright like someone with a fever. When she came out of this state of suspended animation and focused in on Shelley, she leapt out of bed and grabbed her in a bear hug.

"Oh, Shelley, can it be possible? Can it be true? I've lived fifteen years without falling in love, and now it's happened in one magic night. Isn't love wonderful?" Dana danced around the room.

At this Shelley burst into tears.

"Oh, Dana," she sobbed. "I'm sorry. This isn't about you. I'm glad you had a good time tonight. Really I am."

"Something went wrong when you talked to Paul, right?" Dana said, looking for a yes or no answer since Shelley was crying so hard a longer one didn't seem possible.

"*What* Paul? He wasn't even there. The call I've been waiting for all week, he completely forgot." Shelley sobbed loudly.

"Oh, I can't believe he forgot," Dana said, putting an arm around Shelley's shoulder. "He probably just went out somewhere and couldn't make it back in time, or got the times mixed up. All that time zone stuff is confusing."

"You think that's it?" Shelley asked, calming down a little.

"Shelley. I don't know for sure what went on tonight, but I can tell you that boy hasn't fallen out of love with you in just two weeks. There's either some reasonable explanation, or he's got some apologizing to do. But whatever, you two will work it out. This is a small snag, not a major romantic trauma."

"Oh, Dana, you're so smart about this stuff," Shelley said, grabbing a Kleenex to blow her nose.

"Me? Smart about romance?" Dana laughed, tossing her long hair back with a shake of her head. "Believe me, I'm the original babe in the woods. Remember? I'm the one who just fell in love for the first time tonight."

"Oh," Shelley said, remembering the start of the conversation, "that's right." She smiled. "You want to tell me about it?"

"Are you sure this is a good time?" Dana asked, peering closely at Shelley to make sure the tears were really gone.

"Yes. I think it's time I started trying to get out of myself a little. *And* I'd like to start trying to be as good a friend to you as you are to me."

They looked over at Faith, who was sitting up in bed, watching them. "*What* is going on?" she asked sleepily.

CHAPTER ELEVEN

Dana's night hadn't started off on such a high note. She had assumed that either Faith or Shelley or both would go to the mixer. When they finked out, she had to make a choice between not going or going alone. One seemed dismal, the other dreadful.

First she decided to forget the mixer, stay in, and study. But that was just too depressing a way to spend a Friday night. So, when she felt a small burst of confidence after dinner, she went with it and put on her best pair of designer jeans and a tuxedo shirt, threw a green cotton sweater over her shoulders, sprayed herself with L'Air du Temps, and ran out of the dorm before she could lose her courage.

Two other girls from down the hall were also going out the door. She didn't know them that well, but they asked if she was going to the mixer and when she said yes, they suggested all walking over together. She was grateful for the company — at first.

They were Mary Lou Turner and Sally June Barnes. They were from the same town and had been best friends all through grade school. They were freshman roommates at Canby this year. Both were blond, talked the same way — a mix of regular talk and baby talk — and squeaked when they giggled, which was often. They were so alike it was eerie. More alike than sisters — more like clones.

"Aren't you just so nervous you could die, Mary Lou?" Sally June asked her.

"Heart's a-thumpy thumpums," she said, tapping the spot.

Dana couldn't tell if they were being sarcastic. She hoped so, but it was a slim hope.

"What about you, Danny?" Mary Lou asked.

"Dana. It's Dana. I don't know. I'm interested in meeting new people."

"Ooooh, you don't fool us," Sally June said. "Does she, Mary Lou? You mean interested in meeting *boys*. And there are going to be so many of the cute-ums in one place."

"But Sally June," Mary Lou said, "if I don't get asked to dance, I'm just going to die."

"Oh, you'll get asked. Don't worry your head."

The conversation was beginning to make Dana dizzy, as if the altitude were too high and she couldn't get enough oxygen. She had thought that hugging the wall alone, waiting to get asked to dance, would be the worst possible fate, but that was before she had been faced with the prospect of a night hugging the wall waiting to be asked to dance *and* being in the company of Mary Lou and Sally June. She had never thought about it before, but she was suddenly glad she had only one first name.

Dana had been to dances and mixers before back in New York, but she had always gone with friends, and most of these events had been at her school, so she had known a lot of the guys there. This was a different story. Here she was going to know nobody except two girls she was becoming less and less sure she wanted to know at all.

Oakley Prep was just half a mile down the road from Canby Hall. The mixer was being held in the main gym there.

The gym was, well, it was a gym — cinder

block walls, hardwood floors. It smelled like sweat and floor wax. The only decorating that had been done to convert it into a dance hall was that it had been rigged out with red-and-blue colored lights playing over the walls. The kind of thing boys thought was sophisticated. It just made Dana feel like she was inside a jukebox.

One good sign was that there seemed to be more guys than girls. There were already some couples out on the dance floor, but there were a lot of girls in groups like she was. The walls were practically lined with what she guessed were specimens of *Boyus Oakleus* — Oakley Boy.

"Well," Mary Lou said, "I most certainly hope these cute-ums know the latest dances."

Dana most certainly hoped they didn't. She didn't. She was a free-style boogier, which is to say she didn't really know how to dance at all. She just got out there and moved around and hoped she didn't look much more stupid than anyone else on the floor. What she mostly hoped at this moment was that someone would ask her to dance. Right off, she noticed three really attractive someones: a tall blond in a red sweater, an intense-looking type with longish hair, whom she fantasized as a French exchange student, and a truly gorgeous guy with thick black hair and a cleft in his chin.

Apparently her telepathic waves were going out but not in the intended direction because when, a few seconds later, someone *did* ask her to dance, it was none of them. The invitation came from behind, with a tap on her shoulder.

She turned to find herself face to face — well, actually chin to forehead — with a member of the opposite sex who was nearly a head shorter than she was. He also had buck teeth. Oh, well, she thought, so he wasn't the man of her dreams. Sometimes the least likely looking boys had the really terrific personalities.

She never did find out what kind of personality he had. This was the early phase of the mixer. They were playing only rock numbers, and so they danced about three feet apart. The music was so loud that even shouted conversation would have been impossible.

Then, after four or five numbers, he sort of nodded a combined thanks and I'll see you and walked off, which left Dana with an odd feeling. How could it be that she hadn't cared a bit about this person, but now suddenly cared a whole lot that he had walked off without asking her name, or if she wanted another dance, or a Coke? How could she feel rejected by someone she hadn't even accepted? And what was going on with him? What was it about her that he hadn't liked? Or was he just shy and awkward?

Dana often thought that she had no fundamental understanding of boys. They seemed a vast and mysterious subject that would take years to figure out. She thought maybe by the time she was twenty-five she'd do it. Maybe not until she was forty.

She hung around for half of the next song to see if her luck was going to get any better. She gradually edged back toward the wall so she wouldn't look like a complete fool standing in the middle of the floor by herself. Actually, if she had kept dancing in this mob scene, probably no one would even notice that she was minus a partner.

She went out of the gym and wandered down the hall until she found the girls' bathroom. She went in and recombed her hair. She looked in the mirror and thought maybe she should get one of those perms that would give that wild, tangly look Alison had. Maybe she looked too neat and unmussed and prissy. Maybe that's why she was getting nowhere tonight. Then she calmed down and thought she was overreacting a little. She probably didn't need to rush to a phone and call a plastic surgeon.

She stopped on her way back to the gym to get a Coke from the machine in the hall. She drank it slowly, thinking maybe someone would come up and start talking to her, but that didn't happen. Everyone else was either in couples or groups, talking and laughing. Suddenly, coming here without Faith or Shelley seemed way too brave.

She went back into the gym. She thought she'd better let Tweedledum and Tweedledee know she was leaving so they wouldn't think she'd been abducted. She spotted them right away, dancing, of course, right next to each other. Both of them had snagged fairly neat-looking guys. She felt a leaden heaviness in her chest. Here were two of what she thought were the biggest dips she'd ever met and *they* were doing fine here. While she was sinking like the *Titanic*.

As she was thinking this thought and a whole slew of even bleaker ones that followed, the record ended, the red lights went off leaving only the blue, and a slow song came up over the sound system. A disembodied voice from the invisible disc jockey announced that this dance was ladies' choice.

What the heck, Dana thought. Why not go out in a firy blaze of defeat — make the night a perfect failure. She scanned the crowd. Both the blond in the red sweater and the French boy were taken, but amazingly, the gorgeous one with the cleft in his chin was just hanging around on the sidelines, talking with another guy. *Well*, she thought, *why not*? She had nothing left to lose.

She used the same approach that had been used on her — the sneak attack. She came up behind him and tapped him on the shoulder. When he turned, she bowed and said, "May I have the pleasure of this dance?"

He smiled.

"Well, I should check my dance card, but I'm pretty sure I'm free for this one."

It was that easy. She let him lead her out onto the floor and slide her into his arms, and off they went into a blur of blue.

He smelled terrific. Dana couldn't resist the right aftershave. This worried her a little. Was she destined to a lifetime of swooning any time she was within five feet of a splash of Aramis?

The next thing she liked about him was how he danced — smooth and easy, as if it were a way of getting to know her rather than a performance. She hated winding up out on the floor with boys who were trying to be Fred Astaire when she was nowhere up to being Ginger Rogers.

The third thing she liked about him was what he said when he finally said something.

"It's funny you asked me to dance, because I've been watching you since you came in."

"You have?" she said, then was afraid she'd sounded *too* surprised.

"Mmm-hmm. I was just working up my nerve to come over when Gopher got you in his clutches. The next time I looked, you'd vanished."

"You make me sound mysterious," Dana said. *Is this being too coy?* she wondered.

"Well, so far you are. I don't know a thing about you. Except that you're a pretty girl and dance really nicely." No sooner had he said this than she stepped on his foot.

"*And* I've got great timing," she said. They both laughed.

"Where are you from?" he asked.

"Can you guess?" Dana said, then imme-

diately regretted it. Why was she playing
Twenty Questions with him? He was probably going to think she was an idiot and get
away from her just like the first boy had, as
soon as the music stopped.

"Well," he said, "you're not blond, but
you do look like you could be a surfer, so I'd
guess you're a California girl."

"Close. I'm from New York City."

"I'm from Boston."

"Then you probably know my Aunt Harriet. She lives in Boston." She hoped he could
tell she was teasing.

"Sure do," he said. "But then, everyone in
Boston knows Aunt Harriet. She's the toast
of the town."

"It must be because of her cakes. She
bakes great ones." Dana was feeling a little
more comfortable.

"No, actually she's the toast of the town
because of her toast. She's figured out a way
to put the jam on the bottom."

Dana laughed and pulled away a little so
she could look at him. This was easier than
this kind of thing usually was for her. They
really seemed to be on the same wavelength.
If he could make fun of party chatter, he
clearly thought it was as stupid as she did.

"Isn't small talk awful?" she said. "I guess everybody has to go through it, though."

"Not really. We could move right into bigger talk. But I think we ought to go somewhere quieter if we're going to do that."

"Out in the hall?" Dana asked.

"Or better, we could go back to my dorm." He started moving to the door.

"Oh," Dana said nervously.

"Oh, it's not like that. There's open house in the student lounges tonight. You know — punch and cookies. There'll be house staff around to keep an eye on us. I should be safe." He smiled at her warmly.

Dana laughed. "Well, in that case, I guess it'll be all right."

As they walked out of the gym together, she tugged at Mary Lou's sleeve.

"I'm taking off now," Dana said, trying to make it sound casual. But this was like trying to be casual with a barracuda. Mary Lou, while continuing to boogie — grabbed Dana by the elbow and held it while she said loudly, "You vamp you. Pretty fast movesy woovesies."

"Yeah," Dana said, "Well, see you." She knew this guy must have overheard the exchange, and she wanted to go through the floor.

* * *

It had grown cold outside. Dana put her sweater on, then suddenly stopped and turned to him. "I just realized. I don't even know your name."

"Bret. Bret Harper."

"I'm Dana Morrison."

"Tell me more. Tell me all about Dana Morrison." She knew he was trying hard to sound grown-up.

"In twenty-five words or less?" she teased him.

"I think my attention span is good for at least fifty," he said, teasing her back.

"Well, I'm fifteen. This is my first term up here. I've got a mother and father, but not together. I've got a sister. I don't know what else. I don't have any bad habits, except biting my nails."

"Finger or toe?" he asked, smiling.

"Are you going to let me finish? I must have at least ten words left."

"Go ahead," he said, doing a mock bow from the waist and making a flourish with his hand.

"I like to sing," Dana continued.

"And you want to be a rock star," he said smugly.

"No, an architect. What about you?" she asked, really interested.

"Oh, well, I'm in my third year here. I'm from Boston. My family's *real* Boston. My dad's a banker. My mother's a prep school dean. My brother wants to be an architect like you. He's in grad school at Cornell. We have a big old house and an Irish setter and a sailboat we race in the summer. I hate describing myself. I always come out sounding so preppy."

"Are you?" she asked, not teasing this time.

"I'm not sure. Most of the time, I like following in my family's footsteps. They seem to have a good thing going. But I have odd days when I get the urge to punk out, if you know what I mean. I'd like to show up at dinner some night in my tweed jacket and rep tie with my hair streaked purple." He smiled, but his voice was serious.

Dana laughed. "I *do* know what you mean," she said.

By this time, they had arrived at the lounge, where they stacked a paper plate with cookies, got themselves cups of punch, and found a corner away from the other couples. They sat down and talked about themselves, their lives, their families, their hopes for the future, about which rock groups and movies they liked, which books they had read. They agreed on a lot, had fun disagreeing on the rest. Dana couldn't remember ever being so at ease with someone new. By the end of the night, she felt as if she'd known Bret Harper for years.

He walked Dana back to Canby Hall in time for her to make her midnight curfew. They stood on the steps of Baker, among all the other couples saying good night, holding onto the last moments of the evening.

Dana got suddenly nervous. It had been a wonderful night, but now that it was over, what — if anything — would happen next?

He seemed to pick up on her nervousness. He pulled her off to the side, away from the other couples, and put a hand on her shoulder. He looked hard at her. She could see the coach lamps of Baker reflected in his eyes.

"I really had a good time tonight," he said.

"Me, too," she answered.

"I'd like to do it again."

"Ditto," she said. She hoped he'd hear in her voice how much she liked him.

"What about tomorrow night?" he said, and smiled.

"I should be cool, I guess, and say I'm booked," Dana said. "But where does cool get you?"

"They say the movie at the Rialto's pretty good." He took her hand and held it.

"Even if it's terrible, I'd still go." Dana laughed with embarrassment.

"I love girls who play hard to get," he said, then paused slightly before kissing her — very softly. He paused again before turning and walking away. When he'd gone a few feet, he turned and said, "I'll pick you up at seven-thirty. You're not one of those girls who keep a guy waiting an hour, are you?"

"No. I'm boringly punctual," Dana said, yawning.

"I'll bet you're not boringly *anything*," he said, turned again, and took off at a run in the direction of Oakley.

CHAPTER TWELVE

Dear Sarah,

It's cooler here than you'd think. I mean, I thought this place would be a lot of tea and crumpets — you know, ye olde New England girls' boarding school — but it's a lot more hip than that. Like last Sunday, Baker had a brunch at noon. We all dressed up (which is to say we draped a lot of scarves over our sweaters and wore all our junk jewelry at once) and there were white cloths and flowers on tables in the lounge. Four girls from the string section of the band sat in a corner and played chamber music, and we had French toast with powdered sugar and bagels with cream cheese. We were pretty impressed with ourselves. We felt like ladies at lunch.

Some of the girls here are rich and snooty like I expected. They have crew-necks in fourteen different colors with coordinated oxford cloth shirts, and families they can trace back to the boats they come over on (and I do not mean the kind of boats our ancestors came over on). At first I thought Dana was one of them because of all her clothes. But it turns out her mother's a fashion buyer and can get her samples. Most of the girls here are like her — regular. Some are even really poor. The girls are mostly white, but there are blacks and other minorities. They come from all over the world. Big cities. Small towns. Shelley comes from a place that has about 3,000 people. I think we've got more than that in our neighborhood. You'd probably think she was a hick at first, but she's so warm and honest, you forget that after a while. I'm beginning to see that people are a lot the same underneath. If my French gets any better, which seems unlikely at the moment, I'm even considering trying a conversation with Simone, a French girl who lives in Baker — in her language.

I've found a real soul sister here — and she's white! Her name's Casey Flint, and you'd really like her. She's got an offbeat attitude toward this place that keeps me laugh-

ing so hard I forget to be scared sometimes. She's troubled, though. Her parents have pretty much deserted her. I don't know what to say to her about this to make her feel better. I've just been trying to be around because she needs someone to lean on.

Classes are hard. Sometimes it seems every teacher thinks his is the only class I'm taking, so I've plenty of time to do all the work he lays on me. I get back to the dorm at night swamped with assignments. Sometimes I'm afraid I'm not going to cut it. But then, everyone else seems to have the same worry, so maybe nervous is just the normal state of mind around here.

No great romance has appeared on my scene. Shelley's got her farm boy back on the farm. Dana's met someone here. They're both goony in love, which gets a little sickening. Maybe I'm just jealous. There is this guy who takes pictures for the Oakley yearbook — Raymond Dixon. I had to borrow a lens filter from him the other day. He caught my eye, but I'm not sure I caught his. He's pretty much all business. But then, we'll probably have more contact and something could develop (as we say in the photo biz).

I miss you and Mom and Richard and D.C. in general. Some nights I even wish I

could cry. But basically I'm doing okay here
— hanging in anyway. And everything
doesn't seem so strange anymore, just hard.
I guess that's progress. Don't tell Mom I've
got any worries up here. That would only
worry her. And don't you worry about me,
because basically I'm cool.

> Your loving sister,
> Faith

CHAPTER THIRTEEN

Dana sat nervously on the first hardwood pew in the choir loft. She could look down over the railing into the chapel, which she thought was beautiful — so imposing in its quiet way. The walls were white, the stained glass windows framed in wood, the altar plain and flanked by heavy velvet drapes in blue and white, the Canby Hall colors.

She was listening to Becky Gates sing "O Little Town of Bethlehem." In this middle of a mild October afternoon, the song seemed a little out of place. But the Christmas Choral *was* one of the biggest events of the choir's season, so maybe choosing a carol was a brilliant strategy on Becky's part.

This was showdown day. Dana had made

it through the open auditions and the semifinals. Now she was among the four finalists. Still, there were only two spots open in the choir this year. Now she knew how all those Oscar nominees felt, quivering in their tuxes and evening gowns, waiting for the envelopes to be opened.

Someone already in the choir had told her that it was rotten luck to be trying out this year. Last year there had been ten openings and only eight girls trying out. The audition had been a mere formality. If a girl could sing "My Dog Has Fleas" and stay on tune for all four notes, she was in. This year there had been fourteen girls vying for two spots. A lot of them were really good. Dana was surprised she had made it this far. She didn't think she'd make it any farther.

The other finalists were all choir or choral singers and had been in groups back home. Dana's singing had all been on her own, and self-taught. She usually backed herself up on her guitar and sang mostly at parties. A couple of times she had sung in school shows, once in a Greenwich Village coffeehouse where her guitar teacher knew the owner, but that was the extent of her public appearances.

Also, she was used to singing popular songs. In the first two auditions, she had sung "Blowin' in the Wind" and "Michael Row the Boat Ashore." They were about as close to religious music as she got.

Rhonda Taylor was up next. She sang "Santa Lucia." An Italian song — now that was class. It was practically opera. Dana looked over at Mr. Brewster as Rhonda sang and thought he looked impressed. Why hadn't she thought of something like this? Of course, the only Italian song she knew was an old Dean Martin number her dad had taught her. That would have made a *big* impression.

When Rhonda finished, Leslie Swoboda, a big freshman with a huge voice, got up and sang "Just a Closer Walk with Thee." The rafters practically vibrated. Leslie was sure to get in.

Dana was last.

"What've you got for us today?" Mr. Brewster asked.

" 'Amazing Grace,' " Dana said, and handed her sheet music to the organist.

She sang it straight. There was no sense trying to out-country Willie Nelson or sing soul like Aretha Franklin. She'd just sing it like a white girl from New York. She couldn't be anyone else. All she could do with this song was put the best of Dana Morrison into it.

When she was finished, she thought it had gone pretty well. She'd cracked just the tiniest bit on the "me" at the end of the "saved a wretch like me" line. But other than that, she didn't think she'd made any mistakes.

They all looked at Mr. Brewster, who in turn looked absolutely noncommittal.

Mr. Brewster was the ultimate out-of-it musical genius type. Between coaching the choir and the school band and tutoring individual music students, he spent his time writing music. In choir he looked as if he was under a lot of strain at being taken away from his true vocation to deal with twenty-five unruly teenage girls.

He was a skinny man with lots of nervous mannerisms. He wore green sport jackets with blue pants and mismatched socks. Once Dana had seen him leave the teachers' table in the dining hall with his napkin tucked into the waistband of his pants.

So it was hard to guess anything from his blank expression right now. It might mean that he hadn't decided. Or he might know who he wanted but not feel like talking about it at the moment. Or he could be off someplace else — listening to a tuba and oboe duet inside his head. All he said was, "Thank you, girls. I'll let you know in a few days."

A few days! Dana thought they were going to find out today. How was she going to wait even longer in this state of suspense? A *few* days. What did *that* mean? Three? Twenty?

The four of them stayed around for a few minutes after Mr. Brewster left, complimenting each other on their performances. They were all being supportive of each other in spite of the furious competiticn. Dana ducked out as soon as she could. She didn't want to stay long enough to find out that any of the others had trained at Juilliard or had been coached by Luciano Pavarotti. In her present state, she couldn't afford to add one more piece of nervous-making information to her brain.

She couldn't believe how much she wanted this. When she had come for the first audition, it had been sort of a lark. Then Alison had told her that the choir was very important at Canby Hall.

"Plus they go on all sorts of tours. In the

summer, they usually go abroad. Two years ago, they went to Sweden. Last year, they went to Japan."

Then somehow, in all the anxiety over trying out, Dana got caught up in it. She began to really want it. She realized that she was used to getting a lot of what she wanted without too much trouble. This was one of the first times she'd had to really work like crazy for something.

She had planned to run after the audition, but when she came out of the chapel, it was pouring rain, so she just bolted in a direct line for Baker. When she got there, she took off her sweat shirt, pulled it inside out, dried herself off a little, and thought about what to do for the next hour.

She didn't want to go up to the room. Shelley and Faith would be having their French salon. They were both having a terrible time with French. But they had to pass the course, and so they had come up with the salon as a way of boosting each other through. After classes, they sat around the room for an hour or so quizzing each other on vocabulary, conjugating verbs, taking opposite parts in the dialogues in the book.

To put them more in the mood for this, they wore berets and scarves and ate "French" snacks — French fries or French vanilla ice cream — and sprayed the room with French cologne. Dana didn't want to interrupt them, and besides, it was madness to try to get anything done in the middle of that scene. Since she was taking Spanish, she couldn't be much help to them.

She decided to go up and bother Alison. Actually, Alison seemed to like being bothered, especially in the late afternoon when she graded papers from the literature class she taught. Alison liked teaching but despaired of some of her students. She said she could stay sane for about ten papers and then usually ran across one in which a student referred to the "Notsies" in *The Diary of Anne Frank,* or stated that Sir Walter Scott had written the national anthem. This made her fear for the future of literature. She thought maybe rays from television sets had destroyed brain cells in some of her pupils.

Dana knocked on the door of the penthouse. She could hear Janis Joplin singing "Piece of My Heart" from within.

"Who goes there — friend or foe?" Alison called out.

"Me. Dana."

"Definitely friend," Alison said, and opened the door. She was wearing jeans, a plain white Indian cotton shirt, and a thin silver bracelet with tiny pieces of turquoise in it. Dana, who was very attuned to style after years of living with a fashion-buyer mother, liked Alison's a lot.

"Not grading papers?" Dana asked.

"No, I'm giving myself the afternoon off. I was sort of hoping someone I like would drop by and here you are. What's up?"

"I just lived through the final choir try-out," Dana said, getting out of her jacket and flopping down onto the floor cushions.

"From the fact that you're not collapsed in a puddle of tears, I gather you made it." Alison waited for Dana's answer.

"No. I mean I don't know. Mr. Brewster's going to think it over for a few days."

"You'll make it." Alison said, tousling Dana's hair in a gesture of reassurance.

"You haven't heard the competition," Dana said, sighing.

"I've heard you. That's enough. Come on in. You want a Tab? I went to town yesterday and stocked up my goody fridge."

"Thanks."

Alison opened a can for Dana and sat down on the floor cushions with her.

"So. What else is new?" Alison asked, pushing her glasses up on the bridge of her nose, looking hard at Dana. Clearly, she was looking for a real talk, not just an idle chat.

"Nothing much," Dana said evasively.

"That's not what the gossip mill tells me."

"What *does* it tell you?" Dana asked. Although everyone talked about everyone else at Canby Hall, Dana was still surprised to find out someone had been talking about *her!*

"That you and Bret Harper are the hottest new item on the Canby-Oakley social scene." Alison smiled broadly.

"Hey, wait a minute! I only just met him the other night. I've had exactly one real date with him. We saw the new Robert Redford picture and split a small cheese and sausage at Pizzarino's." Dana avoided Alison's eyes.

"Do you like him?" Alison got right to the point.

"Who wouldn't?" Dana smiled, suddenly feeling shy.

"*Who hasn't* would be more to the point," Alison said.

"Are you trying to tell me something?" Dana asked hesitantly, pretty sure she didn't want to hear Alison's answer.

Alison pushed her glasses up on her nose, then hunkered down with her elbows on her knees, her hands together with fingertips touching. Dana could tell she was getting ready to say something serious.

"No. I don't want to give you any big warnings, just some information. Bret Harper's cute and smart and fun, and half the girls on campus would give their eyeteeth to go out with him. I say half because the other half — more or less — already *have* gone out with him. They have a few great dates, and get a rush of wildflower bouquets, clever cards, and illegal late-night calls on the pay phone. Then, just when they're sure this must be true love, they find that Bret has suddenly disappeared from their life. The calls and cards and flowers stop. He's suddenly too busy with homework to go out for a while. Or he thinks things are getting a little too serious, and he needs a little space. And then a week or two later, he's going out with someone else.

"Last year," Alison went on, "I heard a bunch of girls were going to form a club called the Teardrops — all the ex-girl friends of Bret Harper. At meetings, they were going to throw darts at his picture."

"You're trying to tell me he's a heartbreaker," Dana said, beginning to feel a little queasy.

"He seems to like the thrill of the chase," Alison said. "Once he's got a girl, he loses interest. Of course this was last year and the year before. Maybe he's changed completely over the summer. I just thought this was information you should have. If he's up to his old tricks, you'll know soon enough. All I'm saying is don't lead with your heart. I like your heart. I don't want to see it smashed."

"I think it's too late. I think I'm already a little in love with him." Dana's voice was very low.

"*Really.*"

"Well, maybe just infatuated." Dana shrugged.

"But you just told me you've only had one date."

"*And* three phone calls and two cards and a wildflower bouquet," Dana said, and it was the truth.

They both laughed.

"Okay," Dana said. "I promise I'll be careful. Although I must say I've never had my heart broken. If it happens, maybe it'll be an interesting experience."

"Wrong," Alison said firmly.

"It's happened to you?" Dana asked. She was dying to know something about Alison's life.

"Once or twice."

"Bad?" Dana asked, encouraging Alison to go on.

"Once."

"Has it made you bitter?" Dana asked.

"Oh, yes," Alison said. "I'm a tragic figure now. I walk the moors every night in my white gown, searching for Heathcliff."

"Seriously," Dana said.

"Seriously, it's made me more cautious. I think I'm going to ask for references on the next one. And steer clear of poets. But enough about my romantic past. I've got stuff I want to ask you. Like how it's going up in 407." Alison changed the subject.

"Great," Dana said, stretching out on the floor cushions. "I really think we're getting to be each other's best friends. Well, Faith also hangs out a lot with Casey."

"The problem with hanging out with people like Casey is that they're so hell-bent on being bad girls that you run the risk of winding up in the same trouble as they get into. I know Patrice already has her suspicious eye on Faith, which I don't think is justified. How's Shelley doing — is she working through her homesickness?" Alison's real concern was in every word.

"No," Dana said, sitting up. She'd been lying back on the floor pillows, draining the last of the can of Tab. "I think it's getting worse. She didn't get mail from home one day this week, and I found her down in the lobby just standing there looking into our mail slot, as though if she looked long enough, a letter would magically appear." Dana stopped for a minute and retied the lace on one of her running shoes. "And her boyfriend isn't behaving. He was out for their first call. He hadn't forgotten. He told her the next day he didn't think the time of the call was important, that she probably wouldn't mind if it was a day late. She was furious, but it did no good. He just couldn't see it. He hasn't been writing as often as Shelley'd like, and she thinks he's drifting away. It's not just him. She gets depressed think about all the stuff that's going on in Prune Bluff — that's what Faith calls it to tease Shel — all the stuff that's happening there without her. Personally, I think you could skip a year of Prune Bluff and not miss much, but she just really longs to be back there. And she misses her family and her goldfish and — what's that?"

"What's what?" Alison said.

"That small, sweet, fur-covered being coming out from behind that box of records over in the corner," Dana said, pointing.

"*That* is Doby. I found her down by the trashcans behind the building. I was going to call the animal shelter, but then one day went by, then two. This is Day Four and I think, for better or worse, she's my cat now." Alison looked lovingly at the cat.

"She's adorable," Dana said, twitching her fingers to lure Doby — a featherweight ball of calico fluff — out of the corner. It worked. She came tumbling across the room on tentative legs and sniffed around Dana, purring as loud as a toy motorboat.

"She is, isn't she?" Alison said.

Dana stood up suddenly. "Well, I'd better get back down to the French Quarter. And Alison," she said.

"Yes?"

"Thanks for the warning. I appreciate it. But Bret Harper isn't dealing with just *any* Canby girl this time around. He's dealing with Dana Morrison." But Dana didn't feel as confident as she was trying to sound. She had thought Bret was special, that what they had together was going to be special. Finding out about his track record didn't make her want to call it quits with him, but it did shake her up. It also made her sad that she now had to be suspicious of someone she'd thought she could trust.

CHAPTER FOURTEEN

Dana was walking with Bret through the woods north of the Oakley campus. She was deliriously happy, but trying not to let it show too much. So far, none of Alison's dire predictions had come true. Bret called every day. They'd gone to a mixer at Canby Hall the night before — Saturday night — and he'd asked her, when they were saying good night, if she wanted to go for a walk in the woods this afternoon.

"Snitch some extra toast at breakfast," he'd said. "I've got a jar of peanut butter. We can make a sort of picnic."

And so here they were — she with a paper bag full of toast, he with a jar of Skippy jammed into his jacket pocket, both of them tramping leaves underfoot, warmed by the sunshine. She wouldn't have believed that, just a few weeks ago, she had been a diehard city person. All the gorgeous changing colors of the leaves, the woodsy night sounds as she drifted off to sleep, and the crisp air had been very persuasive in winning her over to the merits of nature. Of course, there were still moments when she was dying for good Chinese food.

"When winter hits around here," Bret was saying, "it crashes down all at once. First it dumps three feet of snow, then dives to fifteen below. So when you get a really great fall weekend like this, you've got to soak it up. You're going to have to hold the memory for the next three or four months. I wanted *my* memory to be of you and me here."

"Oh my," Dana said.

"Oh my what?"

"It was a very pretty speech." She had never gotten one like it before. It made her feel like a warm breeze was rushing through her.

"I'd think you'd be used to them. Beautiful big-city girl. I can imagine you going to nightclubs in limos with three or four guys in tuxedos." Bret watched Dana's face.

"Oh, Bret. I'm only fifteen. I went to school. I played my guitar and sang. I ran.

I cooked dinner for my mom and sister a lot."

"No nights on the town with boyfriends?" Bret asked.

"Well, I'm not Cinderella," Dana said. "I did get out of the scullery once in a while."

She was deliberately vague. She didn't want to let him know he was her first real boyfriend. She was working at not letting him know how special he was to her — just in case Alison was right about him. So far, the plan seemed to be working.

And the plan included more than just what she said and *didn't* say. It extended to how she dressed for their dates, like today. She had carefully chosen her oldest pair of jeans, her really broken-in cowboy boots, and a soft and faded chamois cloth shirt. She hoped she looked really good in this outfit, but also like she hadn't gone to much trouble to dress up for him.

She had explained this strategy to Faith as she was getting dressed this morning. Faith's response was typically Faith.

"This is too high-level for my brain. Going to an hour's worth of trouble to look like you've just tumbled out of bed and into your clothes like a fireman. Maybe you should play *really* hard to get — refuse to see him, tell him you hate him, kick him in the shins every once in a while to get the point across." Faith grinned at Dana.

Dana and Bret were deep into the woods. "You want to stake camp here and have our picnic?" he asked. "I want to impress you with what a great gourmet cook I am."

They found a fallen log and sat down. She gave him the paper bag, and he pulled out the peanut butter. He looked at her.

"Where's the knife?"

"What knife?" Dana said.

They both looked at each other and laughed.

"Well," he said after a minute, "I guess we'll have to go really gourmet and have toast chips with peanut butter dip."

So they sat on the log, tore off little pieces of toast, and swiped them into the peanut butter jar.

"You know," he said, "you're a really easy girl to be with. It's like I've known you for a long time and don't have to put on any act at all. I can just be myself. You're special, Dana."

"You're special to me, too. You're the first

person I've ever dipped peanut butter with."
Dana wiped her fingers on the log.

Bret didn't smile at this.

"Why do you always hold me off with a
joke? Don't you take me seriously?" he said,
sounding hurt.

"From what I hear, you're *not* a guy to
take seriously. The word is that you go
through Canby girls a dozen a term." Dana
looked directly at Bret.

"I think I've just been looking for the right
one," he said. "And couldn't find her. Until
now."

As Bret leaned in to kiss her, Dana
dropped her toast, and neither of them noticed when a squirrel scurried up and ran
off with it.

While Dana and Bret were having their
peanut butter picnic, Faith and Casey Flint
were sitting in the Rialto, Greenleaf's re-
vival movie house. They were sobbing
through a tearjerker double feature — *Dark
Victory* with Bette Davis and *A Star Is Born*
with Judy Garland. Casey had already seen
both, so she knew to bring along a whole
box of Kleenex, of which they'd gone through
about half. As they stood by the trash can in
the lobby afterward, emptying their pockets

of crumpled, tear-soaked tissues, Faith said,
"You know, that's the first time I've cried
since I stopped crying after my dad died. It
felt sort of good."

"It does, doesn't it?" Casey said. "I used
to try to tough these pictures out — you
know, hold back the tears to show how cool
I was. But then I saw *Dark Victory* on TV
one night, and it won and I lost. Since then,
I've just figured, why not go with it? That's
what these movies are for anyway — to let
you cry about somebody else's troubles. Make
you forget your own for a while."

"I hope my dad dying is the worst thing
that ever happens to me. I hope my own
life never makes me that sad again. I hope
I never wind up like Bette Davis in that picture — planting my begonias knowing I'll
never live to see them bloom. Or being a
broken-down alcoholic like Lana Turner in
that one we saw last week."

"Where she's in that old hotel in Mexico
with the neon sign flashing outside the window," Casey said, remembering.

"Mmm-hmm. I gues it's not too likely a
fate for me, though," Faith said. "I think you
have to start early to get *there*. I guess, having made it to fifteen without having had
even one drink, I'm probably already too old

to start a real down-and-out life."

"You've *never* had a drink?" Casey was clearly amazed. "Not one? Not even a beer?"

"Nope. Nothing stronger than lemonade. Oh, once at my cousin's wedding, I tried a sip of the punch. I didn't know it was spiked. I spit it out into one of the flower arrangements when no one was looking. It tasted really weird."

"Probably had lime sherbet in it," Casey said. "Nobody with any sophistication goes near punch."

Casey was always saying things like this, making pronouncements on what was and wasn't done in the larger world. Faith had no idea if she knew what she was talking about, but it was interesting listening to someone who at least sounded wise. Of course, she liked it less when Casey's know-it-all attitude slid into ribbing Faith, like now.

"Faith Thompson, swinging black chick, has never had a beer. I can't believe it."

"It's the truth," Faith said, getting a little embarrassed, although she wasn't quite sure why.

"Then I think we're going to have to do something about this hole in your experience," Casey said, smiling slyly. "We're just going to have to have a beer together."

"Just where are we going to *get* this beer?" Faith asked. "I mean, are we going to just go down to Mack's? I know we both look terrifically sophisticated for our age, but I've got real strong doubts, girl, that Mack would just give us a beer without even asking for an I.D."

"Oh, Faithy baby. Sometimes you exhibit so little imagination."

Casey took Faith by the hand and led her into the restroom of the theater.

Faith had mixed feelings about this venture, as she did about Casey and their friendship in general. On the one hand, Casey was exciting, and hanging out with her was guaranteed fun. On the other hand, Casey's idea of excitement was to cruise out onto the edge of trouble. So far, nothing terrible had come of this, but Faith had a feeling it was only a matter of time before Casey would push her luck too far. And if Faith were along with her at the time, it would also be *her* luck that got pushed.

The rest room was, luckily, empty. Casey set her knapsack down on one of the sinks and pulled out her makeup case. She began with an application of liquid base, then blusher, then brushed a thick stroke of blue shadow on each eyelid and over that drew a heavy streak of black eyeliner, pulled out to a catlike point at the outer edges. She pulled out a mascara wand and laid it on so thick that when she was done, she looked like she had false eyelashes.

"Now," Casey said, "a little lipstick." She swiped on a heavy coat of Perfect Peach.

Next she backcombed her curly blond hair until it stood out from her head in wild clumps, then combed it into a smooth, sculptured puff.

"There," she said, turning to Faith. "What do I look like?"

"A country singer."

"Good, that's what we're going for," Casey said, and yanked Faith by the hand.

"This is all going to become clear to me in time, isn't it?" Faith said.

"A very short time." Casey took a slip of scrap paper out of her sack and began jotting down a short grocery list as she walked. When they got to the door of Smyth's Food and Liquors, she stopped before pushing it open.

"Wait out here for a few minutes," she instructed Faith. "When you come in, don't let on that we're together. Just hang out. Buy some chips or something, but keep an eye on me. I want you to see the master at work."

When Faith went in, Casey was already at the checkout counter. She was buying a package of bologna, a loaf of bread, a can of pork and beans, and a carton of milk. She was looking at the scribbled list as the young checkout boy totaled up her purchases on the register. As he was pushing through the last item, the bologna, Casey looked at her list again and said, "Oh, I forgot. My husband said to pick up some beer for him. He's home watching the football game."

"Then he's in for a depressing afternoon," the boy said. "The Patriots are sure to lose today."

"You think so?" Casey said.

"For sure. Say, I'll get you those beers, lady. What's your husband's brand?"

"Oh, no," Casey said. "I can't remember."

Faith's heart jumped into the pit of her stomach. Sometimes Casey was beyond belief. Here she had this guy actually running to get the beer for her and what did she do? — pushed it for the last little buzz of excitement.

"Wait a minute," she finally said. "Budweiser. Is that the one that comes in the red and white cans?"

"Yup," the clerk said. "How many?"

"Oh, I think two'll do."

Outside, on the street, they both doubled over laughing.

"I'm going to nominate you for an Academy Award, girl," Faith said.

They laughed the whole way out of town.

"But where're we going to drink this stuff?" Faith asked when they were halfway back to campus.

"I don't know. What about my room? We can have it with bologna sandwiches. I just happen to have all the fixings. And for our dining entertainment, I'll place a few orders for good old P.A."

Casey could see Patrice Allardyce's front door from the window of her top-floor room at Baker. To fill in boring moments, she sometimes ordered pizza, flowers, a hearse from the pet cemetery, a home whirlpool bath from the rental shop — all in Patrice's name. Then Casey watched through her binoculars as the stuff arrived.

"Do you think she knows it's you doing this?" Faith asked.

"Oh, yeah. She just hasn't figured out the way to catch me yet."

"Sometimes I think I should find a safer

friend." Faith laughed, but at the same time she meant what she said.

When they got up to Casey's room, locked the door, and opened the beers, Faith got suddenly nervous and guilty. What if they got caught? This wasn't small stuff like using the laundry room after hours. This was a major violation of school rules and could get her in deep trouble.

Beyond worrying about getting caught, she was just plain sad knowing how disappointed her mother would be if she could see her now. There she was, back in Washington, working hard to give her kids a start in the world, and where was her darling daughter? Up in a dorm room, avoiding her French homework, sipping on a Budweiser.

When she finished the can, which didn't make her feel much different, she didn't know whether the sour taste in her mouth was from the beer or from how rotten she felt about having done this.

While Faith sat up in Casey's room, Shelley sat alone down in 407. Her afternoon activities had been as follows:

Studied French for half an hour.

Went through Paul's letters with a red marker, underlining the romantic parts.

Ate half the box of brownies her mother had sent that week, then brooded for a while about getting fat.

Cried.

Wrote letters to Paul and to her friend Cindy.

Cried some more.

Drew up a rough draft of the points she was going to make to convince her parents to let her stay in Pine Bluff when she went home for Christmas break.

Took a phone message from Mr. Brewster for Dana.

Took a nap.

When Dana got back from her walk in the woods with Bret, Shelley was still sleeping, but woke up when Dana accidentally dropped three textbooks she was pulling down off the shelf above her desk.

"How you doing?" Dana asked.

"Mr. Brewster called," she said, still half-asleep.

"He did? He did! What did he say?"

"He said you made it into the choir and to tell you the first practice is going to be Monday at four," Shelley said sleepily.

"Hey! I made it!" Dana shouted, and ran over and hugged Shelley. "I can't believe it. I actually made it. Oh, I'm so happy. And Bret's so wonderful. And life's so great. I'm so glad I came here to Canby Hall!"

At this point Shelley burst into tears.

"Oh, Shel," Dana said. "I'm sorry. I'm always doing this — crashing into your feelings. Maybe we could make up a sign. An emotional barometer or something. You could just set it from one to ten, so I'd see how you were doing as I came in and could stop myself from being such an awful friend."

"No. It's my problem. I should be able to be happy for you. What kind of friend am I?" Shelley asked between sobs.

"One of the best, Shel. Really. I'm even thinking of moving Pine Bluff out here. Setting it up next to Greenleaf. That way you could be happy *and* we could keep you around."

Shelley smiled through her tears.

CHAPTER FIFTEEN

Dana got the bad news from Dorothy Hicks, a sophomore soprano who sat next to her in choir. Dana wished she had been placed next to someone else. Dorothy was a terrific soprano, but a really awful person. She was unpopular around school. She had a sulky disposition and greasy hair and bragged constantly about what a big opera star she was going to become. Dana knew enough about psychology to suspect that Dorothy didn't really think she was so great, and just used the opera star line to try to impress everybody. But understanding her still didn't make her much fun to be around, especially since she had clearly decided she hated Dana. Dana didn't know why, didn't really care, except that it made talking with her difficult and unpleasant.

Most of the time, though, they were too busy in choir practice to talk. Brewster worked them like dogs. Today, however, in the middle of practice, he discovered he was missing some sheet music and ran back to his office for it, which left the girls with some time to fool around. Being Canby girls, fooling around meant gossiping.

Dana wanted to get across the choir loft to talk with Elyse Roth. Elyse was a senior and had been friendly with Alison Cavanaugh for the past couple of years. Dana wanted to find out what she knew about Alison's mysterious romantic past, but Dorothy cornered Dana before she could get away.

"Well," she said. "Joe Gennaro finally got around to asking me to the Harvest Holiday. Everybody else had dates by last week. I was beginning to think he was so wrapped up in his trombone that he'd forget the dance completely. He's crazy about me, you know. But he's so in his own world that he forgets little things like the biggest Oakley dance this side of the prom. Who are you going with?"

"I don't know that we *are* going," Dana

said, trying to sound casual. "Bret hasn't said anything about it. I think he thinks big dances are boring. I guess he's boycotting this one. It doesn't matter to me." This was a lie. Dana desperately wanted to go to the Harvest Holiday, and she couldn't imagine why Bret hadn't mentioned it yet.

"Bret?" Dorothy said. "You mean Bret Harper?"

"Yeah," Dana said, and smiled. Lately, she found herself smiling anytime his name was mentioned — the way people just naturally stand up when they hear "The Star-Spangled Banner." "We've sort of been going together since the beginning of the term."

"I guess it's the kind of deal where you date other people, though," Dorothy said, punctuating the statement with a really smug I-know-something-you-don't kind of smile, which really got Dana's hackles up.

"Well, I guess we *could* see other people," Dana said sharply, "but I don't think either of us wants to."

"Hmmm," Dorothy said, as if she were trying to puzzle out one of the great mysteries of the universe. "Then I wonder why he's taking Polly Talbot to the Harvest Holiday?"

"Polly Talbot? That can't be possible!" Dana sputtered.

"Well, I think it's extremely possible. I think it's highly probable — certain, actually. Unless Polly gets sick at the last minute. I ran into her at the florist. We were both ordering flowers for the boys' buttonholes. She's getting Bret a special one."

"Oh, shut up, Dorothy," Dana said, then was sorry. Dorothy was only the bearer of the bad news. It was Bret she was really furious with, and with herself for believing him this past week, when he'd said they couldn't get together because he had to cram for midterms. Dana thought for a minute and managed to come up with a feeble recovery line so she wouldn't have to feel humiliated in front of Dorothy.

"Oh, wait a minute. I forgot that Bret and Polly's parents are good friends. Now I remember. He was saying something about her breaking up with some guy and the families wanting him to try to cheer her up with something. This must be the something."

"But Polly's from Florida and Bret's from Boston. How can their families be such good friends?" Dorothy asked with a slight smile.

"Oh, I think they go skiing at the same resort."

Dana was a terrible liar. She couldn't remember telling a lie this large or this stupid since the time she told a bunch of kids at a roller rink that Paul McCartney was her uncle. That was when she was eleven. She could see that Dorothy didn't believe her and was about to come up with another question or two to try to catch her in her lie. Mercifully, Mr. Brewster bounded in at just that moment with his sheet music and a let's-get-down-to-business look on his face.

Not that Dana had any interest at all in singing now. She was crushed. Alison had been right. She should've listened to her. But she hadn't and now here she was, shot down like a dozen girls before her by Mr. Bret Harper, Oakley Prep's heartbreaker-in-residence.

How could he? Hadn't he meant any of the things he'd said to her? Here she'd been, just floating along on cloud nine, thinking everything was so perfect. Studying for midterms. *Sure*. She should've been suspicious about that.

When practice let out — and it seemed to last three days — Dana ran the paths back to Baker and headed up to Alison's apartment.

Alison came to the door and was immediately responsive to the tears streaming down Dana's face.

"Oh, no. What is it?" Alison asked.

At first, Dana was too overcome with a flood of emotion to speak.

"You don't have to tell me the whole story. Just give me the general topic," Alison prompted.

"Bret." Dana could barely bring herself to say his name.

"Ah," Alison said, looking thoughtful. "Can you give me a few minutes? I've got someone else here right now."

Dana looked past her and saw Pat Adamowski sitting on the floor cushions in the living room, red-eyed and dipping into a box of Kleenex next to her. Apparently Alison was having a run on problems this afternoon.

"I'll wait in the broom closet," Dana said. With three girls to most of the rooms in Baker, and communal bathrooms, about the only places where a girl could get any real privacy were the broom closets on each floor. They got heavy use for deep thinking and major crying.

Dana sat in the fourth floor one for a while. When Alison opened the door, she didn't bother to try to get Dana back up to the penthouse, just put her cup of tea on top of the round vacuum cleaner and handed Dana a cold Tab.

"I thought all that crying might have gotten you a little dehydrated," she said, and sat down opposite Dana. "So, what has the dirty rat done?" Alison asked.

"Asked Polly Talbot to the Harvest Holiday," Dana said despondently.

"Oh. *Major* rattishness. So. What are you going to do about it?"

"What do you mean *do*? I mean, I guess I could kill myself, or become a nun. I suppose I'll just cry for a week or so and then start to forget I ever met the creep." Dana wiped her eyes.

"Is this the Dana I know and love — Miss Spunk herself — just resigning herself to being dumped? Come *on*," Alison said angrily.

"Come on, what? What *can* I do?" Dana pleaded.

"Oh, I think a little light revenge might be in order," Alison said mysteriously.

"Like?" Dana asked.

"You're a creative girl. I'm sure you'll think of something." Alison smiled.

*   *   *

It took Dana a day of hard thinking to come up with the perfect plan and then a couple of hours to talk Faith and Shelley into helping her with it. Actually, Faith was easy. She was used to crazy schemes from being with Casey. Shelley was reluctant at first, but in the end, persuadable. So, by seven o'clock on Friday night, the night of the Harvest Holiday, Plan Booga-Booga was ready to go into action.

Casey had been a help, too. She had a friend in the drama club who managed to get all of them — Casey included (she wouldn't miss a stunt like this) — moth-eaten costumes. The four of them practiced up in 407 after classes Friday, until they got their moves down pat. Then, when the magic hour arrived, they put the costumes into shopping bags, sneaked down the back way, and ran into the bushes on the side of Addison House, Polly Talbot's dorm. Once there, they put on the suits and waited.

"It's getting pretty sweaty in here," Shelley complained after ten minutes or so had gone by.

"Don't worry," Dana said. "It won't be long. It's five after seven now. The dance started at seven. Bret's always ten minutes late — just enough to get you a little nervous, but not so late that you're really teed off."

Bret didn't arrive as soon as Dana expected. He didn't show up until seven-fifteen, but finally there he was. Even in the midst of being furious with him, Dana couldn't help thinking how handsome he looked in his tux. He also had a new haircut, and a long, white silk aviator's scarf tied around his neck. He was carrying a clear plastic box with a corsage in it. Maybe this was a serious thing with Polly, not just a date or two. Dana hadn't heard from him in nearly two weeks. And she hadn't called him. After she found out about Polly, she hadn't particularly wanted to call and find out how hard he was "studying."

When Shelley spotted him coming up the walk, she started to lunge out from behind the bushes. Dana grabbed her furry leg.

"No, Shel. Not yet. Wait until he comes back out with Polly."

Within five minutes, they appeared — Polly with a long pink dress sticking out underneath her coat. She was holding onto Bret's arm, laughing lightly at something he'd said. They were a perfect couple, unsuspecting, and stunned when, as they were halfway down the walk, four obviously fake gorillas leapt out of the bushes at them, bouncing up and down, scratching their armpits and grunting, "Booga-booga."

"Hey," Bret cried. "What *is* this?"

"Probably some club initiation," Polly said, shooing the apes away with the little evening bag dangling from her hand.

"Come on," Bret said. "Joke's over."

"Let's just walk faster," Polly said. But she was wearing heels and so there was no way they could get away from the gorillas. By now, they were getting a lot of attention from other, un-gorillaed couples.

"Whoever you are, would you please just get out of here and leave us alone," Bret begged. "Go bother somebody else."

Further on, he got chivalrous on Polly's behalf, and said, "If you guys don't quit this, I'm going to deck somebody."

At which point Shelley lapsed from booga-boogaing into giggling, thereby giving away the fact that she was a girl.

"Girls," Bret said to Polly. "These are *girl* gorillas. I can't punch out a girl."

Then Polly whispered something to him, which must have been, "Maybe if we just ignore them, they'll go away." At any rate, that's what they started doing — pretending there wasn't a gorilla in sight.

But this did not stop the gorillas, who just continued to swarm around them all the way to the door of the Oakley gym. The four of them were having great fun with this, especially Dana. She loved being able to hassle Bret without him knowing it was her. As time went on, she got so bold in her costume that she finally went one step too far. As Bret was about to go into the gym, she jumped in front of him and gave him a huge, hairy hug.

"Have a lovely night," she said, in her best gorilla baritone.

But apparently her voice wasn't deep enough. Or maybe, with their faces so close together, Bret could see her eyes behind the mask. Whatever the tip-off was, Dana could tell in an instant that he *knew*. She could could see his surprised look of recognition.

"Oh, no!" he said.

Dana didn't wait around to find out what else he might say. She just grabbed her gorilla pals by their arms and shouted, "Time to run!"

Running off into the night, she was glad he had discovered her identity. Let him know it was her. Let him see that there was at least *one* Canby Hall girl whom he hadn't driven to sitting up in her room, sobbing over his rejection.

The next afternoon, when Dana came out of choir practice, Bret was there on the walk outside the chapel door. He was walking in small circles, probably to keep warm, and so Dana guessed that he had been there for a while.

She was walking with some of the girls from the choir and wasn't sure if she wanted to stop and talk to him. But he looked so nervous and shy — so unlike his usual confident self — that he touched her heart. She told the others to go on without her and went over to him.

"Booga-booga," he said, smiling slightly.

"You deserved it," Dana said.

"I know. Will you go for a walk with me? I'm going to freeze to this spot if I stand here much longer."

Dana hesitated, then said, "Okay."

They started off across campus in silence. It took him a while to speak. She could tell he was mentally framing his words. "I'm sorry," he finally said.

Dana was silent.

"I was rotten," Bret continued.

"Yeah, you were rotten, but I got back at

you. Now we're even. So it's okay." She was doing her best to sound casual. She didn't want him to know how hurt she was. It was a matter of pride.

"Would you ever go out with me again?" He was looking at the ground as he said this.

"Why would I want to do that?" she said. "Wouldn't that slow down your march through every girl at Canby Hall?"

"I think maybe it's time to stop that. I know when I've met the right one. I think I knew it all along. But I got scared of my feelings. And so I ran. I guess I just needed a little booga-boogaing to bring me to my senses. When I figured out it was you in that suit, I knew I was really in love. And I knew I'd met someone who wasn't going to stand for me being a jerk."

Dana thought for a moment, then said, "But how can I trust you? How can I know you won't just disappear on me again?"

"I can understand how you feel, but, well, how can I prove I won't if you won't give me another chance?"

She thought for another moment. "I can't, Bret. I'd never feel comfortable with you again. I really cared about you, and you hurt my feelings really bad. I don't want to go out with you anymore. Never!"

Dana turned and ran, hoping Bret hadn't seen the tears running down her cheeks. Bret stared after her, at first silent. Then he called out. "Dana. Please."

But Dana kept running.

CHAPTER SIXTEEN

The next weeks were the hardest Dana had ever been through. She went on with all her usual routines — classes, choir practice, eating, sleeping, talking with her roommates, but there was always a lump in her stomach. Her hands were usually icy cold and the back of every head she saw was Bret's. She would wake up in the middle of the night and lie on her back, staring up at the ceiling, wishing she had never met Bret but glad that she had. She waited for him to call, but he didn't. She hoped he'd send a funny card or a wildflower bouquet, but he didn't.

She lost weight and forgot to wash her hair. The only time she completely forgot about Bret was one Tuesday a couple of weeks before Christmas vacation. Dana, Faith, and Shelley were up in 407 having a particularly mopey night. It had been a hard day for all of them.

It was Shelley's mother's birthday, and she ached to be at home with her family. She looked at photographs from home over and over, sighing loudly.

Dana was depressed. On top of her missing Bret, she had skipped choir practice Saturday afternoon to go to a movie with Shelley. A big mistake. Brewster hated it when anyone was absent. He was so sensitive musically that one missing voice threw the choir hopelessly out of whack for him. And so at that afternoon's practice, he had gotten back at her.

"Apparently Dana thinks she's so good she doesn't need the weekend practice," he said in front of everyone. "Since she's so especially talented, I'd like her to sing a solo piece for us. I won't interfere by playing the organ. The exceptional voice is shown to its best advantage singing a cappella."

She'd had to sing without accompaniment. She had been so rattled that she'd made a complete mess of the song and a complete fool of herself. She was so humiliated that she had slunk out right after practice without talking to anyone. She was *never* going to miss a practice again.

Faith's day had gone fine until she'd brought some film into the *Clarion* darkroom — winter landscapes of the campus that she'd nearly frozen her fingers and toes off to get. Some dolt had mixed up the bottles of chemicals and everything Faith had processed was ruined.

They had all told their tales of woe while they ate Faith's first cooking class project — oatmeal bars. These, unfortunately, had both the taste and texture of door stops and just added to the depressing mood of the night.

By ten, they all decided the best thing to do with a day this rotten was to put an end to it and go to bed. They were sound asleep when someone poked her head in the room and said there was a call on the pay phone for Faith.

At first she stumbled blearily through the halls, but by the time she got down to the phones, her heart was pounding. Ever since her dad had died, unexpected middle-of-the-night phone calls threw her into a panic.

She picked up the dangling receiver filled with fear of what she'd find on the other end.

It was Casey.

"Where are you?" Faith asked, partly relieved.

"At the all-night diner by the interstate," Casey said.

"What *time* is it?" Faith asked. She had gone from sound asleep to complete panic and was just now beginning to come down and focus on the conversation.

"Around eleven, I guess," Casey answered.

"What are you doing out this late? How are you going to get back in here?" Faith asked, confused. "You know we have a ten o'clock curfew weeknights."

"I'm not *coming* back. I'm taking off. I'm going to hitch to California. I've had it with this place," Casey said angrily.

"What are you *saying*? And why haven't you told me anything about this before?" Faith was totally awake now.

"You would've just tried to stop me, and I don't want to be stopped. But I didn't want to leave without telling you. I mean, I don't want to get sappy about it, but you're really my best friend." Casey sounded close to tears.

"Casey," Faith said, trying to think fast.

"What?" Casey's voice was low and shaky.

"Do me a favor. I mean, if I'm really your

best friend, you should be willing to do one thing for me before you go."

"What one thing?" Casey said, suspicious.

"Don't do anything until I can get there. I just want to talk to you. I won't try to stop you. I just want to understand what's going on." Faith's head was spinning. She wasn't sure what she was going to do once she got to Casey. Right now she was just playing for time.

"But how're you going to get out?" Casey asked.

Faith thought for a moment, then said, "Cheryl Stern'll let me use her window. She's on the first floor. I did a portrait photo of her so she could send it to her boyfriend. So she sort of owes me one."

"Okay, okay," Casey said nervously. "But hurry. I don't want to sit here too long or the waitress will get suspicious and call the school."

When Faith got back up to 407, Dana and Shelley were waiting in the dark, but wide awake, to hear the news. Faith told them what was happening, and what she was going to do about it.

"I told her I wasn't going to try to talk her out of it," Faith said, "but I will."

"You'll get caught," Shelley said. "Then you'll be in as big a mess as she is."

"But what else can I do?" Faith pleaded.

"We could tell Alison," Dana said. "Let her in on what's going on and see what she says to do."

"No," Faith said firmly. "Alison's great, but she's part of the authority structure here. She'd have to tell P.A. or risk losing her job. Casey's mixed up, but she's also breaking the rules. Getting her back here before anyone discovers she's gone is the only solution." Faith was pulling clothes out of drawers and the closet as she said this.

"I'll come with you," Dana offered.

"Thanks," Faith said, "but I've got to do this myself. I have to get her to talk, and I don't think she'll do that if anyone else is around. She'd just joke about it, pretend it was another lark. And I know it isn't."

While Faith put on long underwear, heavy corduroy pants, a T-shirt, flannel shirt, down vest and jacket, socks, leg warmers, and boots — Casey had picked one of the coldest nights of the winter to run away — Shelley and Dana stuffed Faith's bed with a person-shaped roll of blankets and robes, in case there was a surprise bed check while she was out.

"Call from the diner so we know what's going on," Dana said.

"I'd better not. I don't want to call attention to this. I'd better just try to talk her back in and see you guys when I get here. Wish me luck." Faith quietly let herself out the door.

By the time Faith got to May's Café, Casey was the only customer in the place. She was sitting in a back booth, her two full knapsacks stuffed in with her. She was nursing what was probably her fourteenth cup of coffee of the night.

"Funny running into you here," Faith said, as she slid into the opposite side of the booth. She didn't want to scare Casey by getting too serious too soon.

"You're being a pain in the neck, you know," Casey said, not looking up.

"I'm trying to be a friend. You'd do the same for me. If I told you I was taking off, you'd want to know why. That's part of friendship — understanding what the other person is about."

"The weather's better in California," Casey said.

"Not good enough," Faith answered curtly.

"I want to break into movies," Casey
stirred her coffee, not looking up.

"Come on," Faith persisted.

"Oh, it's a bunch of stuff. Christmas will
be horrible. My parents will be at parties practically the whole time. I'll hardly see them."
Tears started running slowly down Casey's
cheeks. She kept talking. "I got a letter from
them, too, saying that they're going to
Europe for the whole summer this year. Nobody even mentioned my coming along. Instead they're packing me off to this wilderness camp. You know — one of those places
where you hike about fifty miles a day, then
stop and kill a cougar with your bare hands
for dinner. When you get out, you're supposed to be a better person for having been
so close to nature. And you've got all this
terrifically valuable knowledge, like knowing
how to tie a hundred different knots and how
to tell which are the nonpoisonous berries."

"You could probably talk them out of it,"
Faith said, not really believing it.

"No way." Casey said, still crying. "The
place is supposed to build character and they
think mine is in a bad state of disrepair.
Anyway, that's not the whole of it. Yesterday
the disciplinary board met and I was called
before it. Seems I got enough demerit points

last term for three girls. And so this term I'm on social probation — restricted to campus on weekdays, ten P.M. curfew on weekends. I figure as long as they're going to make me a prisoner, I might as well make an escape."

Faith thought a while before responding. "Running away isn't going to solve anything," Faith said.

"Probably not. But it'll make me feel better. Like I'm *doing* something instead of just letting everyone push me this way and that."

"But this *isn't* doing something. It's just more fooling around." Faith felt angry now.

"You've got a better idea?" Casey said sharply.

"You could start by doing the hard stuff — tell your folks how unhappy you are with them and how they treat you, instead of standing on your head to get their attention. They're jerky to you, so you act like a jerk, and they treat you like one. Somebody's got to break the cycle." Faith watched Casey carefully to see how she was taking this.

"But how?" Casey wiped her eyes with a napkin from the dispenser on the table.

"Well, you could start by taking your medicine here. You act like you're being persecuted, but the fact is you *have* broken three times as many rules as anyone's allowed. So take your social probation. You can use the time to boost your grades. You can make a patchwork quilt. I'll keep you company. It won't be so terrible. Then you can show your folks all sorts of proof of your rebuilt character and put your foot down about the camp." Faith stopped and searched her mind for more encouraging things to say. "I know. If they won't take you to Europe, you can spend the summer with me. My uncle has a small ice cream company. I drive one of the Popsicle bikes. You could, too. It'd be fun to do it together."

"Well," Casey admitted. "The last part sounds good, but everything else sounds hard. I think it'd be easier if I just ran away."

"Casey, I'm trying to be cool about this, but I can't. I'd be scared to death for you if you ran away. I'd worry all the time. So if you haven't got a better reason, you should at least stay on my account. I really *care* about you. So do Shelley and Dana. You're *not* alone here. And you'd really be alone out there. Not to mention how dangerous it'd be." Faith was really frightened now and longed for Alison.

Casey thought a long time. Faith didn't push her. This had to be Casey's decision.

Finally, Casey looked hard into Faith's eyes, put her hand over Faith's, and said, "All right. I'll go back with you. I don't know. Maybe I let you come out here so you *would* talk me out of it. I *was* getting pretty scared. And you're probably right. If I really get my act together, I might be able to get my folks to notice me in a good way. The way I've *been* operating, the only time I get their attention is when they look at me like I'm a juvenile delinquent." Casey stopped for a moment, then went on. "But what if we get caught trying to get back to Baker? Then I'll be in even deeper trouble."

"We won't," Faith said, trying to sound sure of herself, although she wasn't. "Cheryl said she'd wait up for us. We'll just slink from tree to bush until we get there. Then make sure no one's looking and slip in. Easy as pie."

"I know," Casey said, her eyes lighting up. "When we get to Baker, we could scale the fire escape, then lower ourselves on a rope into your window."

Faith let out a sigh. She was exasperated. "Oh, no," she said, "why should we make it that easy? Why not add some *real* excitement? We can break into P.A.'s house and creep up to her room and steal her master

key from the nightstand, then let ourselves
into Baker with it. *Really*, Casey."

"Okay, okay," Casey said. "We'll do it the
easy way."

"Thanks."

When they got back to campus, they began their tree-to-bush-to-tree tactics, which
went pretty well until they had to go past the
headmistress's house. In spite of the lateness
of the hour, there was a light in one of the
upstairs windows. Unfortunately, this was
the one place on campus where trees were
in scare supply. There were only the two
giant oaks on either side of the lawn. They
waited a long time behind the first, watching
to see if Patrice Allardyce was anywhere close
to the window, but they couldn't see her and
so made a break for the second oak.

When they got there, they looked out from
behind it — panting from the sprint — and
there was Patrice Allardyce, big as life and
looking straight at the tree they were hiding
behind. They couldn't tell if she had spotted
them running, or was just having trouble
sleeping and was coincidentally, at this very
moment, looking in their direction.

When Patrice turned and walked away
from the window, seemingly in a hurry,

Faith turned to Casey and saw that her eyes were huge with fright. Faith herself was trembling and knew it had nothing to do with the cold.

"I don't know about you," Casey said, dropping her usual cool tone of voice, "but I don't think we ought to hang around to see whether she's rushing off to bed, or to call the cops. I think we ought to scrap this guerrilla action and just run like all get-out!"

Which they did — all the way to Baker. When they got there, they ran around to Cheryl's window. Faith gave it a push, then a harder push. It was locked. Maybe they had the wrong window. Faith looked inside. There was Cheryl — sound asleep.

"Oh, no," Faith moaned. "And she sleeps like a dead person. There's no way we can get her up without waking the whole campus at the same time."

"Plan *B*?" Casey said.

"Forget Plan *B*, will you?" Faith said impatiently. "Come on. We'll try to signal Dana and Shelley. They can come down and open the window. I *know* they're awake."

They dashed around to the side of the building and began tossing pebbles up at the window of 407. It took quite a while before they could get one up that high. After what seemed like hours of trying, they finally got a bull's-eye and Shelley opened the window.

"Shel!" Faith said, trying to shout and whisper at the same time. "Quick! Get down to Cheryl's and let us in. Sleeping Beauty's locked us out. And Shel — make it fast. We think P.A. spotted us coming in."

"I'm on my way," Shelley whispered back loudly.

Faith and Casey ran back into the bushes outside Cheryl's window. They waited for what seemed like forever until the window finally slid open. Shelley and Cheryl were inside with Dana, who had come along so as not to miss the excitement.

Faith and Casey made a run for it. Casey went through first. As Faith was about to go through, a car pulled in through the front gates of the campus, its headlights sweeping over the lawn. At this hour it could only be a police car from Greenleaf. Faith turned her face away as a searchlight swept over Baker Hall. She felt its heat on her body, and then it stopped its sweeping motion and settled directly on her. Two policemen got out of the car and walked over to Faith.

"You a Canby Hall girl?" one asked.

"Yes," Faith answered, trying to sound calm.

"Kind of late to be out, isn't it?" the other asked, not without kindness.

Suddenly, Faith was aware of another person on her right. She turned her head and looked straight into Patrice Allardyce's cool eyes. Miss Allardyce was in a robe with a down coat thrown over it.

"What is going on?" she asked curtly. "Where have you been, Faith?"

Faith hesitated for one moment and then answered firmly. "I had a date and the time just went by and then it was past curfew. I came back and saw this window open and was trying to get into the building."

"Kids!" one of the policemen mumbled.

Patrice Allardyce turned to the policemen. "Thank you for the fine security you give us. You can go now, though. I will handle this."

Both policemen gave Faith a sympathetic look and got back into their car. Miss Allardyce turned back to Faith. "Be in my office right after breakfast tomorrow morning. We have a lot to discuss."

Faith walked to the front of Baker Hall, knowing that by this time Alison would be up and waiting for the culprit. When she turned the knob of the front door, it opened easily. Alison was waiting for Faith in the front hall, wrapped in a bright red robe and fuzzy slippers.

"Faith," she said, "what happened?"

Faith mechanically repeated her story. "I had a date and then it was late, so I tried to sneak into the building."

Alison looked at Faith dubiously. "Who was your date?"

Faith thought for a moment. "I can't tell you. That would just get *him* in trouble, too."

"I see," Alison said. "I don't believe you, Faith. I don't think that's what happened. It doesn't sound like *you*."

"Well, it's true," Faith said. "I'm tired, Alison. I just want to go to bed." She turned and walked up the stairs to 407. Her shoulders were slumped, and she felt as if she could hardly drag herself up the stairs.

In the room Dana and Shelley sat on their beds. Their faces were pale and their eyes wide. When Faith came into the room, they ran to her and hugged her tightly. Faith was shivering even in her heavy clothes. Dana pushed her onto the bed, pulled a blanket off her own bed, and wrapped it around Faith.

"Where's Casey?" Faith asked.

"She ran up to her own room as soon as she got through the window," Dana said.

"She didn't even wait to see what happened to *you*."

"I have to report to Allardyce tomorrow morning," Faith said, still shivering slightly.

Dana sat down next to Faith. "You *have* to tell her the truth. You have to tell her *why* you were out."

"I can't," Faith said. "Casey's already on social probation, and her parents told her if she gets kicked out of Canby Hall they are going to send her somewhere real drastic."

"That's her problem," Shelley said.

It was so unlike Shelley to say something like that. Faith and Dana looked at her with surprise. "I mean it," Shelley said. "I don't care about Casey . . . only you, Faith."

The next morning, the three girls sat at the breakfast table, pushing the food around on their plates. No one had much to say, until Casey stopped at the table. Her hair needed combing, and her clothes looked as if she had slept in them.

"I'm sorry, Faith. Really. Really."

"You have to tell the truth," Dana said to her coldly.

"I can't." There were tears in Casey's eyes. "I don't know what they'll do to me and what my parents would do to me, if everyone knows I was in this, too."

Shelley looked at Casey with tears in her eyes. "You're really going to let Faith take all the blame for what was your fault?"

Dana reached out and grabbed Casey's arm. "You call that being a friend?"

Casey threw off Dana's hand and said, "I can't tell." Then she walked off quickly.

"She's mean and rotten and selfish," Dana said with fury.

"She's just scared," Faith answered.

"Aren't *you*?" Dana asked.

"Sure I am," Faith replied. "But I have you two and my Mom. Casey hasn't anyone."

"Maybe there's a reason for that," Dana said, still furious.

In Patrice Allardyce's office, Faith sat on the edge of her chair, looking at the headmistress from across her wide desk.

"Let's start again, Faith," Miss Allardyce said. "Where were you last night?"

Faith repeated her story. "I told you. I was on a date and I forgot to watch the time."

"Who was your date?" Patrice asked.

Again Faith said, "I can't tell you. I don't want him to get into trouble."

Miss Allardyce shrugged. "All right, Faith.

As you know, you have seriously broken the rules, not only by missing curfew but then by trying to crawl back into Baker through a window. You will be confined to Baker for a month, except for your classes and meals. This will go on your record and, of course, I will have to notify your mother."

Faith looked up, startled. "Please, Miss Allardyce. I don't mind the first two things, but don't tell my mother. She'll be so upset and worried."

Miss Allardyce rearranged the papers on her desk. "Well, Faith, you should have thought of that before you broke the rules. You can go now."

For the next two days, Faith walked around in a daze. Shelley and Dana tried to cheer her up. They brought her ice cream sundaes and magazines, and joked with her. Most of the other girls in Baker tried, too, dropping funny cards off at Faith's room, buying her silly little inexpensive presents, but Faith remained depressed. Even Ginny Weissberg, appearing one of the days carrying one lovely red rose, didn't bring Faith to say more than "Thanks, Ginn."

The second night, when the girls were in their room studying, the dorm monitor knocked on their door. She said to Faith,

"Miss Allardyce just called. She wants you to come to her house *now*." The girl grimaced. "Why do you suppose she wants to see you, Faith?"

Faith shrugged. "I don't know." She put on her coat, wool hat, and mittens and ran down the stairs, across the cold campus, and into the headmistress's house. Not too many Canby Hall girls got into this house, which was set apart. There were Senior Teas there and brunches for honor students, but the average girl never saw the inside of the head-mistress's home. When Faith walked in she hardly noticed that the living room was filled with cozy armchairs and a flowered chintz-covered sofa. She was barely aware of the crackling fire in the fireplace, which didn't warm her much.

She *was* aware of Casey huddled in a corner of the sofa, crying softly, and Alison next to her with an arm around Casey's shoulders. Patrice Allardyce was standing in front of the fireplace, looking distressed and cool at the same time.

Casey looked up as Faith came into the room. "I had to tell them. I couldn't let you take the blame for what wasn't your fault."

Faith nodded and just said, "Thanks."

"Sit down, Faith," Miss Allardyce said,

motioning to a chair. Then she went on. "Faith, what you did was wrong. You *did* break the rules. But I understand that you thought you were doing the right thing, and you did bring Casey back. What you should have done, however, was to tell Alison immediately."

Then she turned to Casey. "What you did, Casey, was ridiculous. I'm sure you know how dangerous it is for a young person to run off and be on her own in strange places."

Patrice started walking up and down the room, rubbing her hands together. She stopped in front of Faith and looked down at her. "Let's say you didn't know any better."

Faith opened her mouth to say something but stopped when she caught Alison's "keep quiet" look.

Miss Allardyce stood in front of Faith for what seemed to Faith to be an endless amount of time. "I'm not sure what kind of punishment you deserve now." She turned to Casey. "And you, Casey. You're on social probation already. I don't know what to do with you at all. Maybe bread and water for a month."

Both girls looked startled.

A smile crossed Miss Allardyce's face.

"I'm only joking. I know all you girls think I'm a monster, but I'm not *that* bad."

Alison suddenly interrupted. "Do you mind if I say something, Miss Allardyce?"

Patrice motioned for her to go on.

Alison cleared her throat nervously. "Don't you think Casey and Faith have suffered enough already? This has been a very frightening and upsetting experience for them both, and I'm sure they've learned their lesson. For Faith, having her mother know about this has made her unhappy enough."

Miss Allardyce glanced at Faith, who was staring down at her hands. "As it happens, Faith, I haven't written to your mother yet."

A joyous smile lit up Faith's face. "What a relief."

"All right," Miss Allardyce said firmly. "Faith, you meant well though your methods were not very wise. I'll forget this one infraction. It won't be on your record, and I won't write to your mother. I must warn you, though, if you ever repeat anything like this —"

"She won't," Alison said. "I know she won't."

Faith nodded her head vigorously in agreement.

Miss Allardyce looked at Casey again.

Then she turned back to Faith. "You can go now, Faith. Casey and Alison and I will talk a little more."

Faith gave Casey a keep-your-chin-up look and left the headmistress's house. When she ran into Baker House, Dana and Shelley were in the lounge with Ginny Weissberg and Cheryl Stern, all of them waiting. She burst into the room, smiling, and yelled, "It's okay. Casey told them everything. It's all okay."

To celebrate they all donated whatever food they had in their rooms and stuffed themselves with Tab and bagels and peanut butter and marshmallows and pretzels. They all talked at once and cried a little and laughed a lot.

Later, alone in 407 with Shelley and Dana, Faith said, "I'll tell you, for a while there, I felt like a real criminal. When that cop swung his searchlight over me I thought, what would my poor dad the policeman think if he could've seen me then?"

"On the other hand," Shelley said, "if your mom the social worker knew what you did for Casey, I bet she'd be pretty darn proud."

"I don't know," Faith said. "My mom does *her* work through proper channels. I don't know what she'd think about social work that involved midnight runs and hiding from searchlights."

"Don't worry, Faith," Dana said. "You did the right thing. You put yourself on the line for someone else. No one can be a better friend than that."

"I guess," Faith said, yawning. "I ought to get Casey to pay me back by going to my classes for me. I don't know how I'm going to get up at six-thirty tomorrow."

"You mean *today*," Shelley corrected her.

All Faith could do was groan.

CHAPTER
SEVENTEEN

Dana and Faith and Shelley were sharing an ice cream sundae at the Tutti-Frutti after classes the next day. They were intent on getting three spoons into the dish at the same time, when Shelley asked Faith, "Have you seen Casey? Did she tell you what Alison and Allardyce decided to do about her?"

"Yeah," Faith said between mouthfuls. "They had a talk, and Casey's going to get counseling. Alison suggested it, and Casey says if the school wants to provide someone to listen to her rant and rave, it's okay with her. Which I think is Casey's way of saying she knows there's some stuff she needs to work out. Boy, I hope the other night is the most exciting one I have all year." Faith sighed.

"I have to say a lot more happens in

about a week here than in a year in Pine Bluff," Shelley said.

"Do you think *I* could go to Pine Bluff for a while?" Dana asked. "I could use the rest."

Faith gave Dana a quick look. She was almost as good as Alison when it came to sizing up a situation. She knew that Shelley was going back to the room to finish a term paper. "Feel like a brisk walk around campus?" she asked Dana.

Dana shrugged wearily. "It's as good as anything else I can think of to do."

They walked back to Canby Hall and started down one of the paths. Faith reached out and grabbed Dana's arm. "Wait. I don't really want to walk. I want to talk to you."

Dana looked reluctant. "About what?"

Faith moved her head in the direction of an empty bench alongside the path. "Let's sit down here."

"Why?" Dana asked suspiciously.

"Because I'm tired," Faith answered.

"You can't fool me," Dana mumbled, but she sat down on the bench and huddled deep into her down jacket, staring in front of her.

"Dana," Faith began, "why don't you call him?"

"Who?" Dana asked, never moving her eyes from the path in front of her.

"Who? You know who! Bret."

"Never," Dana said firmly.

"You're miserable," Faith said. "So he made a mistake. He said he was sorry. Give the guy a break. Call him."

"Why doesn't *he* call *me*?" Dana asked petulantly.

"Come on, Dana," Faith said with irritation. "You tell the guy to take off and now you expect him to come running after you."

"I was so definite. I told him I'd never go out with him again. How can I call him now?" Dana's voice was low, so low Faith could hardly hear her.

"Easy," Faith answered. "You put the dime in the phone, dial his dorm, and ask, 'Is Bret Harper there?' Then he comes to the phone 'and *he* says —"

"Okay, okay, I get your point," Dana interrupted.

It was eleven o'clock at night. Dana was in her robe and slippers, shivering in the phone booth on the main floor of Baker. It wasn't cold, but she was shivering anyway.

"Is Bret Harper there?" she asked when the dorm monitor answered the phone.

"Do you know what time it is?" the guy asked with annoyance.

"It's important," Dana answered.

Five minutes later, Bret said, "Hello?"

"Can I see you? I want to talk," Dana said hesitantly.

"Any time, any place," Bret answered immediately. "What do you want to talk about?"

"Well, *never* seems like a long time." Dana felt the tears on her cheeks, and her voice cracked.

"Hey, Dana. Don't cry. I really don't want you to cry. I do really love you, you know. Can I buy us a pizza tomorrow night?"

"Sure. I'll meet you at the pizza place at six." Dana felt a great load lifting from her.

"Oh," Bret said. "Just one thing."

"What?" Dana asked.

"Could you wear your ape costume? I'm crazy about girls with hairy arms."

CHAPTER EIGHTEEN

Faith and Dana were in the same sixth-period swim class. Part of the Canby Hall curriculum was one physical education class or team sport per term. Since neither of them had sports of their own — Dana was a solitary jogger, Faith a nonathlete who thought a good workout was a night of changing records on the stereo — they had both decided to take beginner swimming as a way of fulfilling the requirement.

"If we do it together, we can keep an ear out in case the other starts *glub glub glubbing*," Faith had told Dana.

Now they were nearly done with the course and were practicing their freestyle, which was still pretty free-form. Faith, who was nearsighted and usually wore contacts, kept bumping into the end of the pool until the swim instructor, Ms. Barnes, let her start wearing her old glasses in the pool. Faith knew she looked ridiculous and hated how Dana laughed practically every time she looked at her, but it was better than going around with a perpetual bump on her forehead from head-on collisions with solid tile.

Ms. Barnes was running back and forth along the side of the pool, shouting instructions to various girls, especially to Leslie Benbow, who was doing much worse in the course then even Faith or Dana. Leslie looked like a wheat thresher rolling and churning her way across the pool with wild, flailing moves.

Ms. Barnes (her first name, which Dana had spotted on the name tag on her duffel bag, was Rita) had long blond hair and looked more like a surfer than a teacher. She was not laid back like a surfer, though. She mostly conducted the class in a state of mild panic, constantly scanning back and forth over the pool to make sure none of her girls were going under. When her nerves gave out, she just blew the whistle, even if it was, like that moment, ten minutes before the class was supposed to end.

Faith and Dana pulled off their caps and

goggles and headed for the showers. As they stood under side-by-side showers sudsing the chlorine out of their hair, Faith said, "It's really kind of a joke, isn't it? Us doing all this swimming while Shelley sits high and dry — and her the pro. I wonder why she won't go near the water here? She could probably make the junior varsity team easy."

"She knows that," Dana said, "but she doesn't *want* to be on the team here. She wants to stay outside of everything at Canby Hall so she can go home and convince her parents she's been one-hundred percent miserable her whole time here. If she let herself go out for the swim team, she might have a little fun and spoil her image of tragic suffering. Did you bring the blow-dryer?" Dana asked, toweling off.

"I forgot," Faith answered.

"Nuts."

"I'll have to use one of those wall dryers then — the blasters. I hate them. They make me look like the Bride of Frankenstein. Do you think there's something we could do to cheer Shelley up — something not tied up with school?" Dana asked over the sound of the dryer.

"We could cut her hair," Faith said. "It sure could use it."

"I don't think *that* would do it." Both girls laughed. "I think she *likes* her hair that way," Dana said thoughtfully.

"That can't be possible. She's got to know she looks like 1958 with that bubble-do." Faith walked over to the lockers.

"Well, I think now that she's out of the boondocks, away from Pine Barf, it's beginning to dawn on her that her image is sort of in a time warp. But I think she's too depressed to do anything about it." Dana aimed the nozzle of the wall dryer at the back of her head and began running her fingers through her long hair to get the underneath dry. When Dana was done, she went over to Faith at the lockers.

"Why don't we pay some special attention to her?" said Faith, who had apparently been thinking over the Shelley problem. "We could do a makeover on her, like in the magazines. We could cut her hair and get her ears pierced. (Faith herself had one ear pierced with two holes, the other with none. She just wore both earrings in her left ear.) Steal her purple nail polish. Take her over to the shopping mall and get her a pair of jeans that aren't some dumb color. It might give her a lift to change her style a little.

Whenever I'm feeling down, I do something different with my hair or makeup."

"But Faith, how can we do this without insulting her? I mean, when you tell someone you want to make them over, you *are* sort of saying that how they look now is not terrific. And our idea of how she should look might not be hers. If she really is going back to Pine Burp for good, she should probably stay the way she is. Lime green jeans are probably *in* there," Dana said.

"Lime green jeans can't be *in* anywhere," Faith said, sure of herself. "I know we could give her a good revamp. We just have to think of a way to approach her about this. I know — what if I tell her it's part of an assignment in my photo class, styling a model for a shoot?"

"Great!" Dana said. "That's it!"

When Dana and Faith got back from swimming class, Faith sprung the makeover idea on Shelley, being careful to refer to it as a "styling."

Shelley surprised both of them by going for the idea almost right away. The only part she balked at was the haircut.

"I promise I won't take more than an inch off anywhere," Dana said, putting her hand over her heart. "I've been cutting my sister's hair for years. I'm real sensitive. I'd only do a *shaping* on you, not a real cut."

"If you scalp me," Shelley said, "I'll kill you. You'll never know what it's like to graduate from high school, or eat caviar, or go to Paris, or any of the things you're always dreaming about. And I'll have to spend the rest of my life in a maximum security prison."

"Okay, okay," Dana said. "I get the point."

They started the makeover on Saturday morning with a shopping trip to the mall just past Greenleaf. Since Shelley hardly ever went anywhere or did anything, she had loads of allowance saved up. Faith and Dana helped her get rid of a lot of it on a pair of baggy, pleated jeans that did a good job of disguising the chunkiness of her lower body. Then they picked out a crew-neck in a dusty rose and a navy button-down shirt.

They took her to the earring shop, where she got her ears pierced. Over Faith's objections, she insisted on one hole in each ear.

"I'd feel unbalanced any other way," she said. They picked out plain gold studs for her first pair of earrings.

When they got back to the dorm, Dana

began the haircut. She was super-careful as she had promised she would be. She did as light a trim as she could to get the hair all one length all over. Then she set it on small hot rollers to get it really curly. When she brushed it out, it looked much more casual, freer than Shelley's old style.

Faith did the makeup, just using a little blush, mascara, and light lipgloss.

They wouldn't let her look in a mirror until they were all done and she had put on her new clothes. Then they led her down to the bathroom where there was a full-length mirror.

At first she didn't say anything, just stared at herself. Then slowly she started to smile until her grin was as wide as her face.

"You guys!" she said, pulling them both into a three-way bear hug. "You really did it! You've made me into a *Seventeen* model. Really. I hope you get an *A* on the assignment, Faith, but even if the pics don't turn out and you get an *F*, this is still worth it. Am I ever going to knock 'em dead in old Pine Bluff!"

Then she was silent. "Maybe you wouldn't have wanted to do this for me if I'd told you first."

Dana stared at Shelley. "Told us what first?"

Shelley leaned against one of the sinks. "I'm not coming back. I told Alison today. It's definite."

"But your parents," Faith said. "What will they say?"

Shelley turned on the cold water faucet and cupped some water in her hands. She turned to Dana and Faith, after sipping some water nervously. "I called them last night. I told them how unhappy I was, and they said if I was really so miserable I didn't have to come back after Christmas."

Dana gasped. "I don't believe it."

Shelley reached out to her. "I'll miss you both, but I don't belong here. I want to be home with my folks and Paul. I've really made up my mind."

They knew that Shelley meant it. It was in the tone of her voice, in the way she stood, and it was in the way *they* felt, missing her before she had gone.

CHAPTER NINETEEN

Dear Dad,

It was great of you to come up Sunday for the Christmas Choral. I was really surprised to see you. I'm glad you thought I was good, although I can't believe you could really pick my voice out of twenty-five others. But then, maybe fathers have specially tuned nerve endings in their ears.

I wish you could've stayed longer. And I wish you could've met Bret. Shelley and Faith thought you were "neat" (I quote).

And I wish I could've talked to you more at the restaurant, but I was self-conscious in front of Eve. She's pretty. Who is she? I mean I know she works at the agency, but is she just a friend, or is she a girl friend? I don't think she liked me. She kept looking at

me funny across the table. Like I was about
to sprout fangs.

Mom's on a buying trip, or she and Maggie
would've come, too. It would've been fun
having you all come up together. Then you
wouldn't have had to bring Eve for company.
I'm sure listening to a bunch of girls sing
carols couldn't have been her idea of a great
time.

I've got to run. We've got finals next week,
and I'm studying every minute. I even
brought books down to dinner last night, if
you can believe it.

I'll probably be in a state of collapse when
I hit New York. I'll crash at home and call
you when I wake up. And Eve or no Eve, remember we've got a date Christmas Eve.

Love,
Dana

P.S. Shelley isn't coming back after vacation.
I can't stand it, but she wants to be home.
There is already talk about putting some
girl who can't get along with anyone else
in our room. Great.

CHAPTER TWENTY

The Friday before Christmas break was to begin, Canby Hall was a madhouse. Many of the girls were still taking the last of their Term One finals. Those who had finished were in a flurry of packing to make trains and planes and buses home. Room 407 was no less berserk than anyplace else on campus. Faith and Dana were done with their exams and frantically getting their stuff together. They were going to take the same train from Greenleaf to Boston, then change to an express, which would drop Dana in New York and take Faith on to Washington.

They wanted to leap and scream and dance with delight. Exams, and all the tension and studying around them, were over.

Christmas break was beginning. It was a moment for celebrating, but instead, they had to whisper. Shelley still had one final to go, geometry, and was scrunched over her text and notebooks desperately trying to figure out the length of the third side of an isosceles triangle. She was leaving, but she wanted to leave with good grades.

Beyond not wanting to disturb her, the other two were quiet for another reason. In the middle of all their happiness, they were sad knowing that this was the last time they would all be together. This would be Shelley's last day at Canby Hall. Forever.

It was hard for any of them to find the right things to say. Faith and Dana knew how desperately Shelley wanted to be back home, and they were sympathetic toward her. On the other hand, they were really going to miss her, but they didn't want to make her feel bad about leaving them.

Shelley, for her part, was already missing the other two. And, although she still felt she belonged in Pine Bluff, she didn't want them to think her leaving meant that she didn't care about them.

Everyone's emotions were so complicated that they couldn't really express them. So when it came time for Faith and Dana to catch the Canby Hall van to the train station, they pulled Shelley away from her geometric misery and gave her large hugs. Everyone was working at keeping the tone of the moment light.

"Go for it, girl," Faith said. "If you're happier home, you know we're going to be happy for you."

"They are really going to be surprised when they see the new you get off that plane," Dana said.

"I do look pretty neat, don't I?" Shelley said, patting her new hairstyle. "Come on, I'll help you lug all this stuff down to the van."

It was downstairs, standing outside Baker in the wet, cold, gray winter afternoon that all their stiff upper lips disappeared. Faith, surprisingly, was the first to crumble. Tears welled up in her eyes as she said, "Oh, Shel, what've they got back there that you can't get here? Oh, I know a boyfriend and your family and friends and all those cows. I know all that. But *we're* here. What about us?"

"She's right," Dana said, starting to sniffle. "What're we going to do? Who's going to flunk French with Faith? Who's going to crack us up with terrible riddles? What we've got going in 407 is a three-way friendship."

At this, Shelley caught the crying jag that was becoming a minor epidemic.

"Oh, you guys. Don't you think I'm going to miss you, too?" She sat down with a thud on the pile of suitcases and was silent for a minute. Then she looked up at them with the most sorrowful eyes and said, "You two are the best friends I've ever had. But you can come visit me." But they knew they would never see each other again. They clung together in a big hug, and then Dana and Faith ran for the van.

As the van pulled out down the main drive, Faith and Dana wiped the fog from the rear window with their mittened hands and watched as Shelley stood in the slush and waved a limp, sad farewell at them. They kept their eyes on Shelley's blond head and chubby figure as it got smaller and smaller. Soon the only thing they could make out was her red-gloved hand, still waving.

On Christmas night, after two days of gift-giving and holiday dinners (Mexican with her mother, French with her dad), Dana called Faith long distance in Washington.

"Hey, it's me, knucklehead. Merry you-know-what," Dana shouted into the receiver. Faith had picked up the phone amid a lot of background hilarity.

"Dana! You old turkey calling on turkey day. Did you get good loot?"

"A cashmere sweater from my mom. A digital watch from my dad. Maggie and I are *el broko* and so made a pact not to get each other anything. My Aunt Alice sent me a Little Missy baking set. She got stuck a few years back. She thinks I've stayed nine years old. How about you? Did you get good stuff?"

"Yeah, everybody pitched in and got me the lens I wanted. The 28mm. Did you hear from Bret?"

"This morning. *He* got his own windsurfing board. And he says he's restraining himself from making plays for all the girls in Boston."

"I called Shelley this morning," Faith said.

"And?"

"Her mom answered. Said she was on a sleigh ride. No wonder Norman Rockwell's that girl's favorite painter," Faith said. "She hasn't changed her mind. Her mother said so. She isn't coming back."

They were both silent. After a pause, Faith said, "I miss you."

"Ditto," Dana said. "Hey, Happy New Year."

"Yeah. I'll watch for you on TV when they show Times Square at midnight."

"Oh, you know me, I'll probably fall asleep before eleven," Dana joked.

Canby Hall students were due back the Sunday night after New Year's. Early in the predawn hours of that Sunday morning, a foot of snow fell on the patch of New England where the school sat. And so the girls arriving back came in on slow-motion buses, or delayed trains, or waited until Monday in airports where flights to Boston were canceled.

Dana's dad wound up driving her in after they'd waited four hours in Grand Central and had finally given up. He borrowed a four-wheel drive Jeep from a friend so they could make it over the snowy roads.

Faith took trains that were supposed to get her into Greenleaf at two in the afternoon, but it was nearly midnight when she finally got to Baker. She and Dana hugged each other, happy to be together again.

"Whew," Faith said, pulling her boots off and carrying them over to the radiator where she left them to dry. "I was worried I wouldn't make curfew."

"I hear they're ignoring it," Dana said. She curled up on her mattress in a new flannel robe, sipping a mug of cocoa, the picture of coziness.

"I couldn't be sure," Faith said, falling onto her bed. "They're so strict around here, I thought maybe they expected us to parachute in to make it on time."

Once Faith recovered some of her energy, got out of her damp clothes, and stopped feeling like Nanook of the North, the two of them talked and went through most of the box of party mix Faith's sister Sarah had made for them. Shelley's absence hung over them like a cloud. Neither of them brought her name up, though. But her empty bed, the absence of her things on the walls, spoke loudly.

The next day was registration for new classes. In spite of the snow and the fact that the last of the students were still slogging their way toward Greenleaf, things at Canby Hall, if not in high gear, were at least grinding into motion. By late afternoon, both Faith and Dana had registered and gotten most of the classes they'd hoped for.

"I had to take cooking, though," Faith said. "Still life drawing was filled. My only other choices were physics and cooking, which is no choice at all."

"Maybe they'll teach you how to not scorch chicken noodle soup on the hot plate," Dana said.

Faith stuck her tongue out at Dana.

There was a knock at the door, which was odd because nearly everyone at Baker usually just barged in.

"Come on in!" Dana called out.

The door pushed open, and there stood Shelley with snow-covered boots, tired eyes, and a hat falling off the back of her head. She looked like she had come all the way from Iowa on the back of a mule. Clearly it had been a long, rough trip.

"I heard there was room for a third girl here," she said. "I was wondering if you'd take someone from the Midwest."

"Shelley!" Dana and Faith screamed at once.

"What *happened*?" Dana said.

"I know this is going to sound really weird" — Shelley sat down on her bed — "I realized more and more that I didn't really *want* to stay."

"Is it Paul?" Faith asked, narrowing her

eyes, like a detective quizzing a suspect. "Did something go wrong between you two?"

"No," Shelley said quickly, "we're fine. We both think we ought to loosen up a little, though. That we don't have to write every day. We figure that being so far apart, we can't stay attached to each other. We have to live separate lives for a while and hope our love holds anyway."

Shelley took off her coat and hat and scarf and mittens, threw them onto the bed, then flopped down on top of them. She still had her snow-covered boots on but seemed too tired to do anything about them. So Faith and Dana got up and pulled them off for her.

"*They're* all the same. Paul. My family. My friends. It's *me* who's different. They're all just as great as ever, but what they're doing, what's going on back there, isn't *my* life anymore.

"It's funny. All last term, I thought I was just hanging out, putting in my time until I could go home again. But once I got back there, I realized that I'd changed *a lot* here. And it made me sort of an outsider there. Like everyone was real excited about the football team making the regionals again this year. Last year I was real excited about that, too. This time, though, I just couldn't get into it.

"It was like that with everything," Shelley said softly. "I felt like I was standing on the other side of a pane of glass from them. I was there but not *there*, if you know what I mean."

"I *do* know," Dana said eagerly. "It was a lot like that for me, too. It was great being with my mom and Maggie again, seeing my dad. But for the first time, I felt different with them. Before, most of my life was *their* life, too — what they showed me, things we did together. This time, though, I had my own things to tell them about. It was kind of exciting."

"But it's confusing, too, don't you think?" Shelley said. She got up and went through one of her suitcases until she found what she was looking for. "I don't want to keep you two waiting for the crucial ingredient of the evening — Mom's maple-nut fudge."

They passed the box around.

"The other thing," Shelley said shyly, "was you guys. I thought about you a lot. About how much I'd miss you if I didn't come back. Casey, too. Alison. I thought about classes starting up and how if I stayed back there, everything would be happening without me.

Pine Bluff will *always* be my home, but right now I want to be *here*. You guys don't think I'm crazy, do you?"

Faith laughed, then said, "Well, let me ask you this. When you were missing all those wonderful things about Canby Hall, was the food one of them?"

Shelley laughed and made a leap onto Faith's bed and started tickling her. Dana, not wanting to be left out, jumped on top of the two of them.

"Oh, Shel," Dana said, "this is really great! You're not only back, but it sounds like this time you're going to be here for real!"

"Yeah," Shelley said, a little sheepishly, "it looks like somehow, while I wasn't looking or something, I became a Canby Hall girl."

The next morning, when they were dressed and ready to leave the room, Faith pulled her camera bag out of her closet.

"Come on," she said. "Mystery trip."

They followed her along the campus paths. When they got to the front gates, she telescoped her tripod and set up the camera, focusing on the brass plaque that read, CANBY HALL.

"Now that it looks like we're all finally

Canby Hall girls, I thought we should have a group picture for posterity. When we all become famous, they can hang it next to the portrait of Julia Canby in Main Building."

She positioned them a little apart from each other, just beneath the plaque, did a final focus check, set the automatic timer, then jumped out from behind the camera and got between them, draping an arm over each of their shoulders.

"Okay, girls," she said as the timer blinked out its countdown, "say *Canby!*"

As they stood there waiting for the camera to go off, very different thoughts ran through their minds.

Faith was thinking how far she had come from those first scared days here. Now she was the hotshot photographer around campus *and* a second-term sophomore with a B-plus average. She'd made three good friends and pulled one through a serious crisis. *And*, although she was too practical to allow herself to think it would amount to anything, Raymond Dixon, Oakley's hotshot photographer, had called this week and asked her if she wanted to go out on a winter nature shoot with him this weekend.

Shelley was thinking how much her whole outlook on life had changed in just five months. She had gone from being a Pine Bluff girl to being a Canby Hall girl. She also felt that she had become a more grown-up, independent person. Before, she had always thought of herself as somebody's daughter or sister or girl friend. Now she was beginning to think of herself as herself, with choices to make on her own. She still wanted to be a homemaker, to be married to Paul, but she wanted to make the most of her time at Canby Hall. She also knew she wanted to make a good collegiate swim team, which was going to mean lots of hard work during the next two years.

Dana was also thinking about life choices, but different ones. Being in the choir had made her love singing more than she ever had. But if she devoted her energies to that, could she still follow through on all her other plans? Was she going to be able to have everything she wanted in life or was she going to have to give up some things for others? The other thoughts she was having were about Bret and her father. Before Bret, she had thought having a boyfriend would mean dates and flowers and romantic words. She hadn't realized that, between two strong people, it could also be a battle of wills. She wondered if she would be able to have a relationship with Bret and still hang onto her own identity. She wondered about her dad and Eve. Were *they* in love? Were they going to get married? That would put an end to her hopes for her parents getting back together.

These were the thoughts they were thinking as the timer ticked away. When the shutter finally clicked, capturing them together for all time, Dana, Faith, and Shelley were all thinking pretty much the same thing:

Whatever's about to happen, I'm glad the three of us are going to be facing it together!